Catch of the Dead

A Hooked & Cooked Cozy Mystery

by Lyndsey Cole

Connect with me:

Lyndsey@LyndseyColeBooks.com

www.facebook.com/LyndseyColeAuthor

CHAPTER 1

"Do you want the good news or the bad news first?" Ruby asked Hannah as she waved a postcard in front of her younger sister.

"Might as well get the bad news out of the way." Hannah shoved her bills to the side of her big oak desk. "I can't imagine it will be any worse than these invoices I have to pay from all the building materials for my new cottage." She was happy to have an excuse to sort out that mess later.

"Is Cal done? You'll be moving in?" Ruby's face held a glint of excitement.

Hannah sighed and leaned back in her big swivel chair. She locked her fingers together behind her head. Ever since the day she arrived in Hooks Harbor and set her eyes on the ocean front property her Great Aunt Caroline left for her on the beautiful coast of Maine, she had her office in half of Cottage One, where she sat at the moment, with her living space in the other half. To say the least, it was cramped. But that wasn't the biggest problem. The biggest problem was that she felt like she lived in Grand Central Station with guests, friends, employees, and, yes, even her good-looking contractor, Cal, barging in whenever anyone pleased.

"Yes, my new abode is done. I'm christening it—"

"Cottage Five?" Ruby blurted out and laughed. "That fits in with the other original names for your four existing cottages."

"No." She smiled. "I've given this a lot of thought and I've come up with names for *all* the cottages, not just my new one."

Ruby raised her eyebrows.

"I know, it's shocking. My new cottage will be my little paradise—*Slo N EZ*."

Ruby laughed. "Good choice. But I bet you won't be getting much down time to sit back and kick your heels up on the railing of your spiffy porch. After you hear the news I have, you'll be wishing that get-a-way was far, far away instead of only a short dash up the trail behind The Fishy Dish."

A loud groan escaped through Hannah's lips. "I don't like the sound of what's coming; what's the bad news?"

Ruby waved the post card. "It says," she looked at the postcard. "Arriving for a visit on Friday, June tenth."

"That's today!" Hannah almost fell out of her chair. "You've got to be kidding. And they're making time for *us*?"

Ruby scrunched her lips to one side. "Not exactly time for *us*. They want to see the sand sculpture competition which is today. You know, the first event to lead off this big weekend. The judging is tonight. And guess who one of the sculptors is?"

Hannah stroked her cheek. "No clue. Sand sculpting hasn't exactly been on my radar with getting ready for Taste of Hooks Harbor. It's The Fishy Dish's first time getting a tent for that event on Sunday. Who is this mysterious sculptor?"

"Adele Bailey."

Hannah's mouth fell open. Her head slumped forward and landed on her desk with a thud. "Adele that we grew up with in California?" She mumbled more to the desk than to her sister. "If she never came within a hundred miles of us, I could live with that, but you're telling me that she's coming to Hooks Harbor?"

"Yes. As a matter of fact, she must already be here working on her sculpture." Ruby threw the postcard on Hannah's desk and sat on the comfy chair facing her. "Apparently, she's one of three favorites to win, and Mom and Dad want to see her work."

Hannah raised her head off her desk but cradled her chin on her two upturned hands. "Of course they do. She's the daughter they wished they had instead of the two of *us*. What's the good news? I could use something really great right about now to drown this misery that's settling right in my bones."

"I was kidding. There was only bad news and worse news. Mom and Dad will be here later today. That postcard was sent from London three weeks ago but it just arrived so there isn't even any time to get prepared."

"Or flee," Hannah said, knowing that was only wishful thinking. It would be impossible for her to leave with all the responsibility of running her Holiday Hideaway Cottages and The Fishy Dish snack bar.

She hadn't seen her parents in close to two years, and if she was completely honest with herself, just knowing they were coming reopened a painful bag of mixed emotions.

"Did you hear me, Hannah?" Ruby stared at her sister with her eyes opened wide. "You really spaced out there but you better pull it together. I said, Mom and Dad will want to stay here in one of the cottages. I can help you get it ready before Olivia gets home from school."

"Yeah, sure," Hannah replied half-heartedly. "How about you get started. Let's put them in Cottage Four and keep them as far away as possible. Clean linens and towels are in the closet." Hannah stood and squeezed around the side of her desk. "I'll meet you over there in a few minutes."

"Cottage Four? Do you have a new name yet?" Ruby asked.

Hannah picked up a wooden sign and handed it to Ruby. "Cal put two hooks next to the door to hang this on."

"*Something's Fishy,*" she read out loud. "This is eerily appropriate." Ruby rubbed her finger over the ocean-blue lettering carved into the driftwood. "I hope it isn't a foreshadowing for a problem arriving with them."

"What are you talking about? Of course something will arrive with them, and I don't expect we'll like it."

Ruby carried the sign out, leaving Hannah to finish her thoughts about this completely unexpected news. She walked through the door from the office to the living half of the cottage. Nellie, her golden retriever mix, trotted happily behind Hannah. "I think it might be time to open the letter Great Aunt Caroline left for me," she said out loud even though Nellie was her only company at the moment. Talking to Nellie took some of the fear out of what she needed to do.

Nellie woofed.

"That's easy for you to say. I've been dreading finding out what's inside the letter since the day I found it.."

Hannah opened the old trunk inside her closet. She dug under all of Great Aunt Caroline's old clothes and other treasures that she hadn't been able to part with after Caroline died. Her fingers felt the delicate paper envelope and she slid it out carefully. She didn't have to read the now-familiar handwriting on the envelope. *Put this somewhere safe until the day your father arrives – C.*

The envelope weighed very little, but somehow it felt like a stone resting on Hannah's palm as she sat cross-legged on the floor staring at it.

Nellie woofed.

Hannah startled and jerked her head around as her elderly neighbor, Jack, walked in.

"I heard the news. Company's coming?" Jack asked, his voice flat.

He had a habit of showing up at odd times. And, he had been a great friend of Great Aunt Caroline's.

Jack's gaze traveled to the envelope. His brows furrowed. "I recognize that lavender color and the handwriting. I know what it's about." He gently placed his hand on Hannah's shoulder. "I think Caroline would like me to help you with this problem."

Hannah felt her stomach twist into a knot. *Problem?* It had to have something to do with her father. A man she had trouble getting along with after she turned thirteen; always butting heads over the smallest issues. Having a problem with him right now was the last situation she wanted on her plate.

Jack closed the door leading to the office half of the cottage. He rinsed her coffee pot. "I should have brought my own coffee over but this calls for extreme measures so I'll have to compromise and use yours."

Hannah's lip twitched up on one side. She could see that Jack was watching her as he measured coffee and added water into her coffee maker. In his insulting kind of manner, he was actually trying to distract her. And it worked.

"If you only put half the water in, it might be as strong as you like it," Hannah teased as she finally stood and walked to her small kitchen table. The truth was, Jack made about the meanest coffee around, but she had no intention of telling him. She tapped the corner of the lavender envelope on the table. "You make it sound like this envelope contains some type of doomsday news. Do I even want to read what's inside?"

Jack plunked two mugs, cream, and sugar on the table. "You don't have a choice. There's something about your father that only Caroline knew and," he pointed to the envelope, "she hoped you would never have to read her letter."

No one else knew? Not even her mother? Or Ruby? "Why did she leave the letter for me?"

"You are the only one who will be able to stop him, Hannah."

CHAPTER 2

Hannah stared at the words on the envelope and wondered what information could possibly be inside. Her dad and Great Aunt Caroline cut their ties years earlier but Hannah never knew why. It was a forbidden subject.

The thumb on her right hand rubbed over the gold band of the ring Great Aunt Caroline left for her. The motion over the smooth, cold metal always brought her comfort and some other unexplainable sensation.

Just as Hannah inserted her finger under the sealed flap of the letter from Great Aunt Caroline, Ruby walked into Hannah's apartment half of Cottage One. Without knocking, of course.

"Cottage Four is now officially named *Something's Fishy*, the bed is made, and a milk chocolate is on Mom's pillow and bitter chocolate is on Dad's. Anything else need to be done before they arrive?"

Unfortunately, yes, Hannah thought. She dropped the letter and pushed it to one side. She needed to read Great Aunt Caroline's letter, but that had to be done when Ruby was gone. Until Hannah knew what this big secret entailed, the less people in the know, the better.

"That sounds good. Bitter chocolate, though? Where did you find it?"

Ruby rolled her eyes. "Just kidding. They both got a milk chocolate, but I think we should stock up on some bitter chocolate for the future, you know, a passive aggressive way to send a message to unwanted guests." She dropped down on the sofa. "Any plan for when you run into Adele? You know it's inevitable."

"Adele?" Jack asked. "The sand sculptor?"

Hannah swished her hand as if batting away a bug. "Yes, she's here for the sand sculpting event. We grew up with her in California and," Hannah glanced quickly at Ruby, "she's not exactly on our we're-so-glad-you've-arrived-in-our-quaint-seaside-town list."

Jack crossed his arms over his chest. "I heard she could win the competition."

"She always wins, one way or another." Hannah basically spit the words out. "She certainly won our parents' affection. Adele Bailey is Little Miss Perfection in their eyes, and no matter what we did, Adele could always do it better."

"That's right," Ruby added. "Adele lied and cheated every chance she got but, somehow, when she flashed her bright, toothy smile and tossed her head covered with blond perfectly straight hair, no one every called her out."

Jack patted Nellie's silky fur while she sat with her head resting on his knee. "Life tends to catch up with people like that eventually. It sounds like you need to stay out of her way while she's here."

Ruby snorted. "That will be impossible since Dad will include her in everything without consulting us. As far as he's concerned, she's part of the family."

"And she'll twist the knife deeper in our backs as soon as he's not paying attention."

Ruby walked to the door. "I have to pick up Olivia. It's a half day at school today. Oh, I almost forgot. She wants to know if she can sleep over in your new cottage."

"Of course she can. We can pretend we're camping if she wants. I'll hang up sheets for a makeshift tent. Cal made a fire pit for me so we can roast marshmallows, too."

"Great. She'll be so excited. See you back here later?" Ruby kept one hand on the door while she waited for Hannah's reply.

"Definitely. Our only chance is to mount a united front when they arrive."

Jack slid the envelope close to Hannah as soon as the door was closed behind Ruby. "You'd better get this over with so you know what's heading your way. And once you know, you can decide whether to share the news with Ruby. It might be easier if you work together."

"Right." Hannah lifted the envelope. She slid her finger under the glue. The crease of a folded piece of paper burned her eyes.

"Read it, Hannah. It's better to be prepared than to be blindsided," Jack encouraged.

"I know you're right, but it doesn't make it any easier. I know my father and Great Aunt Caroline had a falling out after my grandfather, Great Aunt Caroline's brother, died. That's when we stopped visiting Hooks Harbor and we couldn't even mention Caroline's name. After she died, I thought whatever happened between the two of them would be put to rest. How could I ever imagine that I would be pulled into something I know nothing about?"

Jack sighed. "Caroline hoped that this day wouldn't come. That you would never have to read what's in that letter. But you have no choice now." He touched her arm in an uncharacteristically gentle manner.

Hannah unfolded the paper. Great Aunt Caroline's flowing script met her eyes and she read the words written long before Hannah even knew she would be inheriting this piece of paradise she called her home and now loved more than anything.

Dear Hannah,

If you are reading this letter, it means that your father has decided to show up in Hooks Harbor and push his way back into your life. I hoped this day would never come, but if you are careful and clever, he won't be able to wreak havoc on my legacy to you.

Your father always expected that I would leave my property to him. He cajoled me and threatened me and, as a last straw, he forbade me to have any contact with you, the person I told him would be in my will.

I know he can be manipulative.

You need to know that he always had a goal of using my property, now yours, as the setting for a luxury hotel that only the wealthiest of the wealthy would be able to enjoy. My cottages and snack bar would be leveled under his plan. That cannot happen. They must remain simple, low impact, and available for many to enjoy.

I don't know how he will meddle, but I am one hundred percent positive that if he shows up on your doorstep, that will be his goal.

You must not allow him to get control of this wonderful spot. Stay vigilant and expect danger to show up when you least expect it.

I trusted you with this legacy because I know you have an inner strength to do what is absolutely the right thing.

Do not let your down guard.

Do not be afraid.

Ask for help when necessary.

Love,

Caroline

Hannah read the letter again before she handed it to Jack. Her mind swirled. How could her father get control of the property from her? It didn't seem possible.

Never mind the overly dramatic warnings. *Don't be afraid?* Afraid of what?

Jack read the letter. "I wouldn't worry about this too much. I think Caroline must have been concerned before the property was in your name. What could your father do now?"

Hannah swiped her finger across her upper lip, wiping away a bead of sweat. "That's exactly what I was thinking." Although, if she was honest with herself, her father was clever and she was glad for this warning. Just in case. Her father would never get his hands on the beautiful ocean front property as long as Hannah had a breath in her body.

She steeled her shoulders, pushed a few stray hairs behind her ears, and stood. "I have a business to run, and Meg is probably wondering where I've been. I hope she isn't too swamped with customers at the snack bar, plus the extra planning for Sunday's Taste of Hooks Harbor."

Jack chuckled. "Meg will complain regardless. It's her nature. But you know she's as loyal to you as Nellie is. If you're father does try anything, he'll have to get through her first."

Nellie woofed at the sound of her name.

Hannah followed Jack and Nellie outside. "We've been focusing on my life, but don't you have something to share, Jack?"

He turned toward Hannah. His cheeks were suddenly a shade of pink that Hannah had never seen on his face before. "What are you talking about?"

"Shelly Vaughn? Rumor has it that you've been spending an awful lot of time at her house." Hannah tried to keep a big grin from erupting across her face but she lost that battle.

"Meg told you, didn't she? She can't keep her mouth closed if it's stuffed full of a handful of her hand cut, cooked-to-crispy-perfection French fries."

"Don't try to change the subject. It's about time you've started to enjoy the company of the opposite sex. I don't know why you felt you had to keep it a secret." Hannah linked her arm through her friend's. Even though at least fifty years separated their ages, Hannah and Jack had a close friendship.

"It's Pam." Jack shook his head. "You know my daughter. She's testy in the best of times and I don't think she can handle me seeing someone since her mother died. Shelly and I are friends. That's it. It's enough for both of us. But Pam will jump to all sorts of conclusions and make my life miserable."

"Give her some credit. She's a grown woman and she should be happy for you." Hannah jiggled Jack's arm as they approached The Fishy Dish.

"She should be, but I'm afraid that's not how Pam will see it. You know she still doesn't like you much." Jack sighed as he reached to open the back door leading into the snack bar's kitchen. "No, I'm afraid Pam wants to be the only female in my life."

Meg, Hannah's cook and right hand helper at The Fishy Dish, turned around at the sound of the squeaky door. "About time. Someone's been sitting outside asking every five minutes when you'd be here, Hannah. She's a doozy."

Hannah peeked through the kitchen door overlooking the big deck with the ocean beyond. She saw long straight blond hair. "Great. It's Adele. I wasn't expecting to see her this soon."

Hannah's stomach churned.

"Who is she?" Meg asked.

"A part of my past that I was hoping would never find me in Hooks Harbor."

CHAPTER 3

Without giving herself a chance to change her mind, Hannah pushed through the door of the snack bar kitchen and walked toward Adele who sat fidgeting with her sunglasses at a table outside under the bright sun.

"Jeez, where have you been?" she asked as soon as Hannah came into her line of vision. "Aren't you supposed to be running this place?"

It would have been nice to hear *Hi, Hannah. Haven't seen you for a while. You sure do have a nice place here.* But Adele was all about Adele.

She continued without waiting for a reply from Hannah. "I only have another five minutes before I have to get back to my sand sculpture. I took a break because your father said he'd meet me here." She stood and put her hands on her hips.

Hannah was annoyed to see that Adele was even prettier than she had been in high school. Her long hair, hanging halfway down her back, was that golden-blond color that comes from plenty of time in the sun. Her skin glowed with a healthy tan over a perfectly smooth surface, and a silver mermaid necklace glistened above her pink tank top. The scent of sunscreen wafted to Hannah's nose.

"Well? Have your parents arrived yet?" She rubbed her silver pendant between her thumb and forefinger.

"I haven't seen them yet. They didn't exactly fill me in on their minute by minute schedule." Or even their day to day plans, for that matter.

"Well, tell them I had to get back to my work. They can find me at the beach next to the marina. I'm sure they'll want to see my sculpture since your father told me that's the reason they're coming to this speck-of-dust town anyway."

"Sure. I'll let them know." If I remember, she added to herself.

Adele started to walk away but stopped and turned back toward Hannah. Her eyebrows scrunched together as she gave Hannah a full-body scan. "Oh, you put on a few pounds since I saw you last. Not flattering."

Hannah felt her mouth fall open but she quickly closed it. She didn't want Adele to have the satisfaction of knowing she managed to get under her skin with a twist-of-her-knife-blade insult.

She felt an arm encircle her waist and she managed to relax a couple of her tense muscles.

"Don't listen to her. She sounds like an entitled, spoiled brat." Cal, Hannah's boyfriend, whispered in her ear. The air from his words tickled her cheek. "You're perfect just how you are."

Hannah leaned against Cal's strong chest. "Thanks. And you hit the nail on the head with your analysis. I should know better than to let her goad me but I'm a little out of practice since I haven't seen her for about ten years."

"Close your eyes and take a deep breath of this salty ocean air. That will clear away all toxins, even those that come packaged in the body of a mermaid."

Hannah let her eyelids close. She breathed in deeply and exhaled slowly. Cal was right; concentrating on a cleansing breath sent all thoughts of Adele Bailey out of her system. For the moment.

"Now that you've taken care of that problem, come on up to see your new abode. I think you'll be thrilled with the final result."

"Can I move in today?" Hannah asked, her excitement soaring.

"Uh-huh."

"Perfect, because I'm having a sleepover tonight."

Cal wiggled his eyebrows. "I like the sound of that." He took her hand and led her up the path to the new cottage.

"I don't want to disappoint you, but someone else is coming." Hannah had to jog to keep up with Cal's long strides.

Cal's bottom lip pouted out as he looked down into Hannah's upturned face. "Should I be worried?"

"Only if you're afraid of a little competition from an energetic six-year-old who wants to roast marshmallows and sleep on the floor."

Cal laughed. "Oh, and I'm sure Olivia will be bringing Theodore with her."

"Of course, that stuffed bear goes everywhere with her. I never knew Theodore would be her dearest companion when you entrusted him to her." Hannah remembered how Cal had helped Olivia through a sad time by sharing his thirty-year-old childhood bear with her. Olivia took the responsibility of caring for the bear very seriously.

"Close your eyes," Cal instructed Hannah as they approached her new cottage.

She dutifully put her hand over her eyes but did leave a small sliver for peeking. Her heart raced with anticipation.

Cal held her elbow and guided her up the stairs onto her porch. He turned her around. "Sit." After she was comfortable, he said, "Open your eyes."

Hannah lowered her hand but didn't open her eyes immediately. Instead, she relaxed and let her other senses take over with the call of seagulls filling her ears and the ocean's salty breeze filling her nose.

When she finally opened her eyes, an uninterrupted view of the ocean spread out for miles. Waves made their steady race to shore. The seagulls she heard now swooped through the blue sky, dancing on the wind currents. In the distance, boats chugged along, barely visible. Everything fit together in perfect harmony. Could it last, she wondered?

"What do you think?" Cal asked with an unmistakable twinge of concern.

Hannah pushed herself on the hanging swing. The back and forth motion seemed to be timed with the ocean surges. "This is my paradise, my *Slo N EZ* little paradise."

"Want to go inside?" Cal held his hand out.

"I could sit here all day and enjoy this peaceful feeling with the hope that nothing would ever happen to end it." She stood, knowing that was an impossible wish. "I had a bit of disturbing news this morning."

She rubbed her fingers on the ocean-blue lettering—*Slo N EZ*—carved into the sign as they walked inside. Cal waited for Hannah to continue.

"Ruby just found out that our parents are coming to Hooks Harbor."

"That's bad?" Cal asked.

Hannah had never told him too much about her parents, only that they were traveling all the time.

"The visit itself is stressful but there's more. Great Aunt Caroline left a letter for me to read in the event that my father showed up here."

Cal and Hannah stood looking out the big window of her new living room. "She warned me that my father could try to take this property away from me." She held up her hand to keep Cal from interrupting. "I know it sounds impossible, but I know my father and he never gives up on what he wants."

"Take the warning with a grain of sand, pun intended," Cal grinned at Hannah. "Caroline wrote that letter before she died and she couldn't know how events would evolve after you moved here. This paradise is yours, and if I know anything about you, no one will take it away."

Hannah leaned against Cal. "Thanks for the vote of confidence. My brain tells me that's what makes sense, but my heart is filled with dread and it's hard for me not to have some uneasiness surrounding this weekend. My father and Adele Bailey are a hard combination to fight against. They drain my energy."

The screech of an excited little girl and the thump of sandals hitting the front porch made Hannah forget her worries. She bent down and scooped her niece off the floor and twirled her around in circles. "I hear that someone wants to have a sleep over."

"Yes. Theodore is so excited to come and visit. And me, too," Olivia added as if her teddy bear could visit Hannah on his own.

Everyone laughed. Cal nudged Hannah and leaned close to her ear. "Just think of Olivia when you start to have a stressful moment this weekend. She'll put a smile on your face and recharge your batteries."

Hannah nodded but decided dreaming about Cal with eyes that rivaled the blue of the ocean and hair that matched the sandy beach would relieve her stress even better.

"I'll bring over pizza and beer tonight if you let me hang out with you girls at your campsite," Cal suggested.

Olivia jumped up and down. "Yes. I want cheesy pizza and Theodore likes that, too. But I don't like beer." Her bottom lip turned down into a grimace.

Cal patted Olivia's head. "I'll get you some lemonade along with that cheesy pizza. How does that sound?"

"Yay!" Olivia danced around the empty space. "Where will we build the tent, Aunt Hannah?"

That presented a problem since there was no furniture to drape sheets over. "I'll surprise you. By the time you and your mom get back here, I'll have it all set up. Just bring your sleeping bag and your toothbrush. Come back at six."

"And Theodore," Olivia reminded her aunt. "He's really looking forward to a sleepover."

Ruby rolled her eyes after Olivia ran past her to the porch. "I swear, she thinks that teddy bear is real."

"He is to her and it's not a bad thing." Hannah wrapped her arm around her sister's waist. "I'm heading over to the sand sculpting event to try to head off Mom and Dad showing up here when I least expect them."

"Like tonight when you're enjoying your new cottage?"

"Exactly. I had a visit from Adele not too long ago." Hannah pulled her braid over her shoulder and rubbed her fingers on the silky ends of her hair.

"And?" Ruby stopped and turned to face Hannah. "There must be more to that comment."

Hannah shrugged. "Nothing worth repeating."

"Come on, Hannah. Tell me what you two talked about."

"She told me my extra pounds aren't flattering, and the only reason Mom and Dad are coming to Hooks Harbor is to see her. She hasn't changed one iota, or maybe she has. She has probably matured into a more self-centered, full-of-herself, entitled brat than we ever knew when we all lived in California."

"Wow. Don't mince any words," Cal said with a tone that implied he hoped to lighten Hannah's mood. "Can you use her to your advantage somehow?"

Hannah's face bloomed into a grin. "Of course. That's the perfect suggestion. Since Mom and Dad are here to see Adele, and they didn't give us any notice, we'll have to explain we are already tied up for the evening. Unfortunate, but unavoidable," Hannah added with a mock sad face.

They all stood on Hannah's porch and drank in the peaceful view. "As far as they know, I'm still living in Cottage One. I'll get them settled into their cottage, *Something's Fishy*, and they'll be on their own with Adele."

Olivia was already halfway down the path to the snack bar with Nellie faithfully at her side.

"That sounds like a good plan," Ruby agreed. "For now, I'd better catch up with Olivia and get her home for a late lunch. We'll see you at six, sharp. Hannah?" Ruby rested her hand on Hannah's arm.

"What?"

"This is important to Olivia. Please don't get sidetracked with anything else."

"Nope. I'll get some furniture moved up here." Hannah glanced at Cal and he nodded. "We'll have my new living room transformed into the best sleep over space she could imagine."

Ruby smiled. "Sounds perfect. Good luck with Adele." Ruby jogged after Olivia and they disappeared down the road to their house.

"I take it you're hoping for some help moving furniture?" Cal walked beside Hannah.

Hannah bumped her hip into Cal. "I'm so glad you can read my mind. Let's start with a couple of chairs. That can be my foundation to hold the sheets for our tent."

"Our tent? I like the sound of that." Cal returned the hip bump. "Camping is kind of romantic. Even if it's in your new cottage instead of in a real tent."

"Well, don't forget, there won't be much romance with a wiggly six-year-old and her teddy bear jostling for space between us."

"At least I've finally managed to be included in the overnight part. I wasn't sure if I was allowed to crash this all-girl party."

"It's the least I can do with all the help you'll be giving me for the next hour."

"And don't forget the pizza and beer contribution," Cal added. He opened the door of Hannah's half of Cottage One and followed her inside. He looked at her belongings. "One hour? To move all this?"

"Only what we need for tonight. I don't want it to look empty and tip off my folks. They can think I still live here and I'll be safe in Slo N EZ. We'll get a few things in the new cottage, then I'm off to the beach to see what's going on with the sand sculpting."

Cal picked up one of Hannah's comfy chairs. "I heard that Rory Duff is the hands-down favorite to win the competition. You know, the home boy thing and all. And his girlfriend has made no secret of the fact that the prize money will be their ticket out of town."

"That won't sit well with Adele. She never loses when she sets her focus on something. I doubt she even cares about the money; winning is her game. Rory definitely has his hands full if he expects to win this competition since Adele has more tricks up her sleeve than a magician."

CHAPTER 4

Before Hannah and Cal left for the sand sculpting event, they managed to make a cozy sleepover space in her new cottage. Using two chairs, a small table, and lots of sheets, they transformed her mostly-empty cottage into a magical wonderland that any six-year-old would love. Cal attached two thin ropes to the ceiling to act as the frame and Hannah attached pink sheets with clothes pins. A few glow in the dark stars plus strings of fairy lights on the ceiling created an enchanted indoor sky for when it got dark. A big blanket was spread out next to the tent for their picnic area, and Hannah brought her special bag of toys to play with until Olivia went to sleep.

When they arrived at the beach, it was packed with tourists. All of Hannah's thoughts of her sleepover with Olivia flew out of her brain. As soon as she saw Adele putting the finishing touches on her sculpture, her blood pressure soared. She hated to admit how lifelike the sand mermaid appeared with its individual scales, long flowing hair, and sly grin as it rested with one elbow on a wall of carved stones.

Another sculpture, beyond Adele's, that caught her eye, captured the essence of Hooks Harbor. A lobster boat with a trap and several lobsters inside drifted on a wave carved on the beach.

"Hannah, come over and take a look at Rory's creation. He's sure to win." Jack waved to Hannah as he stood with his arm resting on Shelly Vaughn's shoulder.

Cal leaned close to Hannah and whispered, "Is that Jack's new girlfriend?"

"He says they're only friends." Hannah waved to Jack and dragged Cal closer.

Rory worked with a focus that Hannah envied. Nothing distracted him while he worked. Not even his gorgeous girlfriend, Karla Vaughn, who stood with Jack and her grandmother.

Jack introduced Hannah to Shelly and Karla. Hannah knew the two women from around town but had never formally met them.

"Spectacular work," Hannah said to Jack.

"He has to win unless this competition is rigged." Karla pulled her long hair into a pony tail to keep it from blowing in her face. "We're planning to move to Boston with the prize money. Rory wants to set up a studio and sell his work to a gallery. I'll waitress or something like that to pay the bills. Anything to get out of this town."

Shelly frowned at her granddaughter but remained quiet. Hannah suspected that Shelly wasn't crazy about her granddaughter running after a sculptor with little money even if he had talent. But Hannah also knew it was easier to follow a dream when you were young and naïve. And, who knew, maybe it would work out for Rory. He had to try and let the chips fall where they may. But, it was also foolish to make extravagant plans with money that was *not* in their hand yet. Home boy or not, the judges would choose the best sand sculpture.

Cal tugged gently on Hannah's arm. "There's another artist farther down that has quite a reputation. Let's wander along and check him out."

As they walked along the water's edge, Hannah's eyes scanned the crowd for her parents. She'd rather see them first instead of having them surprise her.

"This guy's name is Moe Meyer," Cal explained when they stopped in front of a stunning scene. "He's from Florida and I heard he and Adele have a relationship of sorts."

Hannah's eyebrows shot up. "Adele has a boyfriend? Now Moe's got my attention. He has no idea what he's in for with Adele."

The scene before them looked life-like. A shaggy-haired young man balanced on a surfboard on top of a big curling wave, all sculpted from sand. Hannah looked at the artist and saw the resemblance to the sand figure. The big difference was the real person had a cigarette hanging from his lips as he worked.

Moe stopped carving for a second to flick his cigarette in the sand.

"Hey, that's littering," Hannah said.

Moe slowly turned to look at her. "The ocean will wash it away."

"You're kidding, right? Pick it up." Hannah glared at the jerk. "Here in Hooks Harbor, we take pride in keeping our beaches clean."

Moe rolled his eyes but he did bend over and pick up the butt, shoving it in the pocket of his cut-off denim shorts. "Any more rules I should know about?" His sarcastic tone was impossible to miss.

Cal put his hand on Hannah's arm. "The most important rule is to enjoy your visit," he said before Hannah could throw out an insult.

Moe laughed. "That's my plan—enjoy my visit and win this competition. Your hometown boy doesn't have a chance."

Hannah felt her blood boil but she clamped her jaw. No point in getting into an argument with him. Instead, she'd wait to congratulate him when he *lost* to Rory. She smiled at the thought of rubbing his loss in his face.

They walked to the end of the sand sculptures before turning around and heading back toward the marina. Cal needed to stop at his boat for a shower and change of clothes before meeting Hannah at her new cottage for pizza and the sleepover.

Hannah watched Cal disappear down the ramp to his boat and she knew she had to quit procrastinating. She had to find her parents before they barged in on her evening.

With thoughts of Great Aunt Caroline's letter about her father, she dug deep inside to find the strength she needed to face whatever agenda he might arrive with. Would he try to kill her with kindness or injure her with insults? He was a charmer with words and Hannah was thankful for the warning from Caroline. At least she knew to be prepared for *something*.

"Hannah! We've been searching all over for you." A familiar voice surrounded her.

"Mom." Hannah accepted the hug. The pressure of her mother's arms gave her strength and she realized how much she had missed the comforting embrace. Joanna Holiday had always been the parent offering unconditional support even when Hannah faced conflicts with her father. Unfortunately, she couldn't have one parent without the other.

And the other was right behind Joanna. "Hannah. We've been wondering when you would show up to see Adele's work. Isn't it fabulous?" Luke Holiday didn't offer a hug or even eye contact. His focus was one hundred percent engrossed with Adele and her sand sculpture.

"Well, I'm here now. Your postcard didn't arrive until today. I couldn't just put my life on hold at the last minute." Hannah didn't hug her father. Why bother? Luke Holiday was already spouting about Adele this and Adele that, leaving Hannah on the back burner of his attention.

"Oh yes, your life. So wrapped up with Caroline's business. What a weight around your neck. She didn't do you any favor, did she?" He finally looked at Hannah, his piercing dark eyes prying into her thoughts.

Hannah ignored her father's comments but the hairs on her neck stood up with the mention of Great Aunt Caroline's cottages and snack bar. Luke didn't waste any time revealing the direction his visit would take.

He laid a heavy hand on her shoulder. "You've reserved one of those little cottages for us, I hope. Your mother and I are counting on staying close to you, Ruby, and Olivia."

"Yes. I'll get you settled in, but we have plans tonight that I couldn't cancel at the last minute so you'll be on your own."

"No problem." Luke glanced at Adele. "We've got plans, too. We're taking Adele out for a celebratory dinner after she wins the competition. Of course, we hoped that you and Ruby would join us." He shrugged. "But if you can't, we'll catch up tomorrow."

"Yes, dear," Joanna said. "I can't wait to tell you all about our travels."

Hannah smiled on the outside. Inside, she cringed. It was always all about their travels. What about Hannah for a change? Whatever. She refused to let herself be disappointed by their lack of interest in *her* life. After all, it was nothing new. She would get through this visit and get back to her life which had settled into a busy but satisfying rhythm around her business and her new friends that supported and encouraged her. Unlike her parents.

Hannah couldn't miss Adele's satisfied grin as she stood behind Luke and stared at Hannah. She smiled back, hoping Adele couldn't sense the hurt Hannah was feeling. Of course it was difficult no matter how much she prepared herself for their visit.

"It sounds like you have a busy evening planned, so how about I get you settled into your cottage while I have some free time," Hannah suggested.

"Joanna, you go with Hannah and get the key. I think I'll wander around here to make sure Adele doesn't have any real competition. I heard there are two other talented sculptors but I can't imagine their work can even hold a candle to Adele's."

"What are your plans, Dad? Sabotage the other work?" Hannah couldn't resist the dig.

A shadow passed over his face before he addressed Hannah's comment. "I doubt anything like that would be necessary. Adele will win without any interference."

Luke turned his back on Hannah and she knew the conversation was finished. She was fine with that. "Come on, Mom. I'm sure you'll want to get back here as soon as possible."

Joanna followed Hannah to the Holiday Hideaway Cottages, pulling her rental car next to Hannah's old Volvo station wagon she'd inherited from her Great Aunt Caroline along with the cottages and snack bar.

They stood together looking at the view. Having her mother alone might give Hannah a chance to find out if her father had an ulterior motive during this visit, as Great Aunt Caroline's letter predicted.

"What do you think?" Hannah asked her mom. "Isn't this about the loveliest spot you could imagine?"

"It's very nice, dear. But isn't it too much work for you?" Joanna tilted her head and looked at Hannah. "Wouldn't you rather sell and use the money to travel?"

"Absolutely not! Great Aunt Caroline left this to me because she knew I would cherish it as much as she did."

"Oh, pish-posh. Caroline is dead. What can she do now? Your dad would love to help you make some real money from this property."

Hannah's stomach twisted into a knot the size of one of the bowls of chowder from her snack bar. She didn't have to wonder anymore. Caroline was right; Hannah had to be on guard to protect her piece of paradise. And not just from her father.

"I'll get the key for you." Joanna followed Hannah to the office and waited outside while Hannah got the key. They walked together, silently, along the path to *Something's Fishy*. Something certainly was fishy and Hannah was worried to find out what.

With chit chat at a minimum, Hannah showed the cottage and watched as her mother returned to her car and left.

Hannah gathered a few items from Cottage One, called to Nellie, and retreated to her new sanctuary. Cal arrived shortly after, surrounded by an aroma of tomato sauce, garlic, oregano, and cheese. Hannah's stomach rumbled.

By the time Olivia dashed toward Hannah's new cottage, followed by Ruby, Hannah and Cal were comfortable on the porch swing, enjoying a cold beer.

Nellie barked a greeting to Olivia but the little girl only had eyes to see inside Hannah's cottage.

"OOOOH," Olivia said. Her eyes were round as she took in the scene. The lights on the ceiling twinkled and threw little star shadows over the pink sheets. "OOOOH," she repeated after she stuck her head inside the tent. "Can you keep your cottage just like this forever and ever, Aunt Hannah?"

The adults laughed. "Not forever, but maybe for the rest of the weekend."

Ruby hugged Olivia. "I'll see you in the morning." She thanked her sister for a night off from mom-duty and headed back to her house.

The evening went well, especially if you were six and the center of attention. After eating too many roasted marshmallows, when Olivia's eyes could barely stay open, Hannah read her a story about a little girl named Sal and her adventure picking blueberries. Olivia never heard the end of the story.

Hannah and Cal talked for a while after Olivia was fast asleep. It was mostly Hannah discussing her parents' visit.

She yawned and stretched. "Let's figure it out tomorrow. I don't want to ruin this pleasant evening." She lay on her back and looked at the lights shining through the pink sheets as she tried to drift off to sleep.

She tossed and turned and finally gave up. A short walk under the stars to the beach helped Hannah clear her brain. Once she returned to the makeshift tent and closed her eyes, it felt like only minutes before the first rays of the new day peeked through Hannah's window early on Saturday morning.

Her back was stiff when she rolled over. The pad on the floor helped cushion her body about as much as a piece of plywood.

The sound of thumps on the few steps leading to her porch caught her attention and she pushed herself up on her elbows. If it was her father, she'd burrow back inside her sleeping bag until he left.

It was Jack. He didn't knock but he cupped his hands around his face and peeked through the window of the door. When his eyes met Hannah's, he motioned for her to come outside.

If it wasn't one thing, it was another. What was Jack doing on her porch so early in the morning? The plan was for them to meet at eight for coffee and cinnamon buns. It was barely even six yet.

Hannah slid from the tent as quietly as possible. Olivia had her arm around Theodore, her mouth was partly open, and her eyes moved in her dream under her closed lids. Cal opened one eye, then the other, and raised his eyebrows. "Where are you going?" he whispered.

Hannah pointed to the porch. Cal soundlessly followed.

Jack paced back and forth on the porch. His hands were shoved deep into his pockets. His normally-groomed white hair stuck out in every direction. "There's been a murder," he said as soon as Hannah stepped onto the porch.

She shook her head, wondering if she'd heard him correctly. "A murder?"

"Yeah. One of the sand sculptors is dead. Shelly's granddaughter found her when she was running on the beach this morning."

"A her? Adele Bailey?"

Jack nodded.

"Murdered?" Hannah couldn't get her head wrapped around what she just heard. Adele—tan, beautiful, and annoying—dead?

CHAPTER 5

Hannah and Cal sat on the porch swing and Jack took a seat next to Hannah. She couldn't go anywhere with Olivia still asleep, not that there was anywhere to go anyway. But it was hard to sit and wait for more news.

"How did you hear about Adele already?" Hannah asked Jack.

"Karla called 911 when she discovered the body, then she called her grandmother, and Shelly called me. She thought I might know more since Pam was the first officer on the scene, but even though Pam's my daughter," Jack shrugged, "she hasn't shared anything with me."

"Of course not. She can't."

"There's more," Jack said.

Hannah and Cal looked at Jack. "More?" they asked at the same time.

"Pam took Rory to the police station. Now, Karla is a complete wreck thinking it's all her fault for finding the body and calling the police."

"If it wasn't Karla, it would have been someone else. But why take Rory in?" Hannah had a sinking feeling. She knew Rory expected to win the competition. Did he take matters into his own hands and kill Adele? Did

Karla help so they wouldn't lose the prize money for their escape from Hooks Harbor?

"Rory and Adele had a terrible argument after she was declared the winner of the sculpting competition last night. He came in second and he went ballistic. In front of everyone."

"So Pam thinks Rory killed Adele to get her out of the way? That seems way too obvious."

"I know. But Rory's shovel was found next to Adele's body." Jack leaned on the railing. His knuckles turned white as his hands gripped the board. "It's the murder weapon. Shelly begged me to help Rory but I don't know what I can do." He turned around and looked at Hannah. "Can you think of anything?"

"Let's wait and see how this develops. Maybe Pam is only questioning Rory. There must be other suspects. What about the other top sculptor?" Hannah looked at Cal. "What was his name? The guy I yelled at for throwing his cigarette butt on the beach."

"Moe Meyer. But I heard he and Adele were dating."

Hannah shrugged. "Maybe something went wrong. Adele was never particularly faithful when I knew her. She liked to toy with her boyfriends, make them squirm, push them away and reel them back in. It was all about control to her. If she did that to Moe, maybe he had enough and snapped."

"Let's not get ahead of ourselves and start accusing innocent people," Cal said. "Talking and being organized about who has a motive and opportunity is a good place to start."

"I hate to say this, Jack, but what about Karla? She already had plans to move to Boston with that prize money. Maybe she decided to take matters into her own hands and get Adele out of the way so Rory would get the prize money." Hannah remembered Karla's excitement and passion when she talked about moving out of Hooks Harbor.

Jack scrunched his mouth to one side. "Shelly thought of that, too. I think that's why she's so frantic. Karla can be head strong and she doesn't always think things through before she jumps in with both feet."

"A definite quality that young people have," Hannah said. It wasn't very long ago that she packed her bags and moved from California to Hooks Harbor, to take over the business her Great Aunt Caroline left to her. When you're young, you don't know what you don't know which can be a good thing. But in Karla's situation? Maybe it turned into something deadly.

It was low tide. The sun glistened on the ocean. From her porch, Hannah watched a few early risers as they ambled along the beach at the water's edge, bending down now and then to pick up a shell or sand dollar or smooth sea glass. It never got old to search for treasures in the sand. Sandpipers skittered away from the walkers, racing toward the water and away again.

Hannah sighed. "I have to spend time with my folks today. They were having dinner with Adele last night, so maybe they'll know something that could help shed light on all of this. Adele was a talker—well, bragger—so everything needs to be taken with a grain of salt, but maybe she told my folks her plans for the rest of the night. If we can make a timeline of her activities, we'll know who had the *opportunity* to kill her. Motive is another thing."

Jack looked at Hannah, his eyes dull with worry. "Thanks, Hannah. Anything to help. I have a feeling Pam will barely talk to me since she's not crazy about my friendship with Shelly. Now, with this problem? I think she'll be gloating with an I-told-you-so attitude. I need to keep my distance."

Hannah nodded. "You know Pam and I have never been particularly close, either, but I'll keep my ears open and let you know what I hear."

"I'm going to Shelly's house now if you need to get in touch. She doesn't know where Karla is and she's afraid her granddaughter might disappear into thin air if Rory ends up being charged with murder."

"Karla is supposed to help my sister, Monica, at the library book sale today. This weekend is always a big fundraiser for them with the sculpting competition, and Monica can't handle the crowd by herself. I don't think Karla will back out of that commitment." Cal ran his fingers through his sandy blond hair. "Karla is depending on Monica for a reference when she moves."

Olivia wandered onto the porch, holding Theodore by one paw, which effectively put an end to the conversation about Adele's murder. "I don't feel good." Her eyes drooped and her shoulders sagged. "Can I go home?"

Hannah crouched next to her niece and pulled her close. "Sure, Olivia. Too much pizza last night?"

"I think so. I ate Theodore's piece, too."

Hannah tried not to laugh. "I'll get my flip-flops and walk you home. We'll leave your sleeping bag right here for another time."

Hannah slipped a long sleeve t-shirt over Olivia's head and flipped her long brown hair to the outside. "There you go. Now your sandals and we'll be on our way."

Nellie wagged her tail, ready for a walk. Cal closed the cottage door. "I'll see if Meg needs any help in the snack bar until you get back." He winked at Hannah.

Hannah and Olivia walked hand in hand, down the road to Ruby's house with Nellie leading the way. Hannah was glad her sister and niece lived close to her Holiday Hideaway Cottages and The Fishy Dish snack bar. Ruby helped out when she could, and Olivia loved to spend her days playing near the beach with Jack and Nellie keeping an eye on her.

The aroma of coffee hit Hannah's nose as soon as she stepped through Ruby's front door. "I hope you have a mug ready for me and maybe some juice for Olivia."

Ruby's face popped around the corner of the kitchen door. "You're a bit earlier than I expected. How was your night?"

Olivia hugged her mother's legs. "I've got a tummy ache."

"Oh dear." Ruby glanced at Hannah over the top of Olivia's head. She raised her eyebrows.

"She ate Theodore's pizza, plus her own," Hannah explained. "Other than that, we had a great time, right, Olivia?"

"Uh-huh. There were stars on the ceiling."

Ruby picked up her daughter. "You can lie on the couch while Aunt Hannah and I have our coffee."

Olivia closed her eyes as soon as her head hit the pillow.

"Too much excitement," Hannah said as she followed Ruby into the kitchen.

"Talk about excitement. Have you heard about Adele?" Ruby set a basket of warm muffins on the table.

"How did you find out?" Hannah sipped her coffee. Bad news certainly had a way of spreading faster than water at high tide.

"Mom texted me. They are completely devastated. She said they had dinner with Adele and, after, she planned to play pool at the Pub and Pool Hall. Isn't that kind of a dumpy place?"

"Meg's brother owns it and all the locals hang out there. That might be a break for finding out information about who she was with and when she left. Jack asked me to see what I can find out."

"Oh?"

"Pam took Rory Duff in for questioning. The local favorite to win the competition. Apparently, he had a big scene with Adele after she won."

"He's a suspect?"

"Looks that way. Jack told me that Karla, Rory's girlfriend, found Adele, and Rory's shovel was next to her body."

"Complicated. What was Karla doing on the beach so early?" Ruby rinsed the dirty mugs.

"Running. It does seem odd, but maybe that's her usual schedule. Something I can ask Jack about."

"Maybe Karla's the one who whacked Adele with the shovel."

"Why would she use her boyfriend's shovel?"

Ruby shrugged. "Are shovels all that different? Maybe she didn't know it was Rory's?"

"Good point. She's supposed to be helping Cal's sister at the book sale today so I can ask her some questions then." Hannah stood. "Thanks for the coffee. I'd better get back to The Fishy Dish before Meg thinks I've abandoned her. Plus, I'll have to meet up with Mom and Dad today. At least you have an excuse with Olivia not feeling well."

Ruby smiled. "I hadn't thought of that silver lining in Olivia's tummy ache, but I'll take it. Sorry to abandon you with them."

"I'm sure you are." Hannah playfully punched her sister in her arm. "You owe me big time."

Hannah and Nellie walked briskly back to The Fishy Dish. Cal had all the outside tables cleaned and the umbrellas opened which was super helpful. Inside, Meg had her don't-mess-with-me face on.

"This weekend is shaping up to be full of unexpected drama," Hannah said as she put away the washed pots in the dish drainer.

"So I've heard." Meg dumped her hand-cut potatoes for fries in ice water to keep fresh until lunchtime. She leaned on the counter. "Listen, Hannah, I know you have a lot on your plate with your parents here, moving into your new cottage, and now this murder, but I can't handle this snack bar by myself. Is Ruby coming to help?"

"She'll be over later." Hannah hoped Olivia's tummy ache didn't last too long. "Jack is tied up with helping Shelly Vaughn stay calm. Her granddaughter found the body. Samantha should be able to help."

Meg rolled her eyes. "Samantha? I guess she'll be better than nothing. Barely. But won't she want to put her ancient private eye techniques to work helping you? I know she won't be able to stay away from this murder."

"Good morning, dears."

Hannah turned her head. Samantha, wearing denim capris, a turquoise blue t-shirt, a big straw hat over her silver curls, and carrying her big canvas tote sashayed into the kitchen.

"Perfect. Can you help Meg until Ruby gets here?"

"Of course. Where are you off to?" Samantha shoved her tote under the counter. She picked a bright blue apron covered with lobsters off the hook and tied it around her waist.

"I need to talk to my parents about their dinner with Adele Bailey last night. Her body was found this morning."

Samantha's eyebrows shot up under her bangs. "A murder? And you expect me to stay here in the snack bar?" She started to untie her apron.

"Just until Ruby gets here. Don't worry, I'll keep you in the loop once I know more. If you want to help, stay here for now. Pretty please?" Hannah even put her hands together as if praying would convince Samantha to work in the kitchen instead of search for clues about a murder.

"Okay." Samantha let out a big breath to show her displeasure.

Meg turned back to her huge pot of clam chowder simmering on the stove. "We need more coleslaw, Samantha. Can you manage that?"

Hannah headed out the door before Samantha had a chance to complain about her latest assignment. She sucked in a lungful of the salty ocean air as soon as she was outside. Who knew her weekend would involve jumping from one fire to another?

"The tables are all set. I raked the sand and swept the deck. Anything else you need help with?" Cal asked as he came up behind Hannah and wrapped his arms around her waist.

"How about you transport me to the other side of all this drama? Do you have a magic wand for that?"

"If I could, it would be the first task on my list. You and me in my boat sailing off into the sunset. But not today. I noticed your folks sitting on the porch of their cottage. I doubt they'll stay there for long."

"I've procrastinated long enough. I'll get this over with. Wish me luck." Hannah leaned against Cal's strong chest before she stepped away and walked along the path to her parent's cottage—*Something's Fishy*.

"Good morning," Hannah said as she approached. Her mother put a marker in her book and set it next to her chair.

"Nothing good about today, or haven't you heard since you're too busy running Caroline's business?" Luke said to Hannah with daggers shooting from his eyes.

"I did hear about Adele. But I don't know anything other than she's...dead." She leaned against the porch railing to one side of the chair her mother sat in. She didn't want to be heartless, but after the way her father had treated her for so many years, Hannah couldn't help but enjoy watching him suffer.

"We had such a nice dinner with her last night," Joanna said. "I can't believe something like this happened to her. Who would do that?"

"That local boy, that's who," Luke spit out. "He couldn't accept that Adele's mermaid sand sculpture was far superior to his old lobster boat. I heard the police already have him in custody."

Hannah cocked her head to one side. "How did you hear about her death? You aren't exactly part of the local grapevine."

"On the early morning news. What a thing to start my day with." Luke stood and towered over Hannah. "That boy will pay if it's the last thing I do for Adele. He's going to rot in jail."

Hannah stared at her father. He already had Rory marked as guilty just a few hours after Adele's body was found. That was typical. It was what he wanted to believe, so in his mind it had to be the truth. Tie it all up quickly without considering any other possibility.

Hannah was absolutely determined to prove her father wrong—if it was the last thing *she* did for Rory.

CHAPTER 6

It wasn't even twelve hours since Adele Bailey was found dead, and the rumors flew faster than a lobster trap could sink. As Hannah searched the crowd on the town green for Karla Vaughn, all she heard was gossip about Adele.

One story had Adele buried beneath her mermaid sand sculpture and another person insisted that she wasn't actually dead but the body was an imposter mermaid in her place. The only thing everyone seemed to agree on was that Adele was beautiful and what a tragedy she wouldn't get the prize money. This was completely out of control.

As Hannah navigated through the mob of people and the tents set up for local craftsmen, she kept her eyes peeled for Cal. They had agreed to meet here. Fortunately, his tall frame stood above most people and Hannah made a beeline toward his blue eyes scanning the crowd for her.

"Can you believe all this crazy talk about Adele?" Hannah asked when she reached Cal's side.

He shook his head. "That's not the worst of it. From what I'm hearing, everyone has Rory pegged as guilty. Have you talked to Karla yet?"

"No, she looks swamped at the used book tables. Once there's a break, I have to find out what she actually saw this morning."

Cal held Hannah's arm and guided her farther away from the crowd. "You have to consider the possibility that Rory *is* guilty. After all, if it's true that it was his shovel that is the murder weapon, well…"

"I know what you're thinking, Cal, but at this point I want to consider all possible suspects, their motives, and their opportunity. If Pam is focused on a quick wrap up of this murder, and she arrests Rory, she may overlook something important. The truth is important to me." To prove my father wrong, she added silently.

Cal tilted his head. "Does this have something to do with your father?"

Did he read her mind? Hannah scrunched up her mouth and looked away. "He has it in for Rory. I don't want him to be right."

"I'll help you, but you have to be smart and careful. Tell me this—" Cal waited for Hannah to look at him. "Why does your father think Rory is the murderer? Could he be deflecting suspicion from someone else?"

Hannah's eyebrows shot up. "He loved Adele like a daughter and wants justice for her. I'll know more after I talk to Karla." Why indeed, she wondered. Her father was a complicated person. Was there some twist in his motive that could hurt her?

Cal interrupted Hannah's thoughts. "It looks like Karla might have a minute to talk. I'll keep my sister busy so you can grill Karla. Good luck."

They walked together to the book tables. Karla glanced up when she saw Hannah. Her bloodshot eyes gave away her grief.

Hannah picked up a book. Ironically, it was a murder mystery. "Do you have a minute to talk?" Hannah asked.

Karla glanced at Monica but Cal, true to his word, had diverted his sister's attention. "Sure." She took the book from Hannah and moved to the far end of the table.

"Listen, Karla, I knew Adele years ago. I heard you found her this morning. What happened?"

Karla looked down. She shook her head as she spoke. "Honestly, I don't know. Ever since I stumbled over her this morning, I can't think straight anymore." She looked into Hannah's eyes. "I don't even remember calling 911. And then Moe was next to me. He sort of took over."

"Moe? The other sculptor was there when you found Adele?" Hannah hadn't heard this tidbit yet and she didn't know what it meant. But it was certainly interesting.

"Right after I found her body, I guess. I was doing my normal morning run and there she was. Dead. Next to her mermaid sculpture. It was almost life imitating art in a weird way."

Hannah patted Karla's shoulder. "This must all be unreal, but it's important to remember every detail." Hannah needed to be careful not to push Karla and have her put her defenses up. She wanted trust to build. Karla could be the most important person to help find out the truth behind what involvement Rory did or didn't have in connection with Adele's murder. And Hannah hoped it was in the *not* connected column.

"I keep going over and over every footstep this morning but I feel like I'm missing something important." She held onto Hannah's arm. Her deep blue eyes pierced into Hannah. She whispered with a quiet desperation, "Rory didn't kill Adele. He's too kind and gentle. He's an artist, not a murderer."

Someone jostled Hannah and she realized it was getting busy at the used book table again. "Can we talk more when you're done here? I don't think Rory is the murderer either and I want to help."

Karla nodded. "I'll be done in an hour. I'll meet you at the marina." Karla looked at the book in her hand. "Do you want to buy this?"

Hannah had forgotten all about the book she picked out. "Yes. Of course." She didn't have much spare time to read, but Cal had built a bookcase in her new home and this would be a start to filling it up. She paid Karla and tucked the book into her tote.

As she moved away from the table she smelled the unmistakable odor of cigarette smoke wafting through the air. She whipped her head around.

Moe stared and grinned at Hannah as he enjoyed his cigarette. What was his agenda? His expression told her that there was more to him than met the eye. He dipped his head in greeting.

This was awkward but Hannah swallowed her pride and approached the cocky beach bum sculptor. She decided to be direct. "What happened to Adele?"

Moe blew smoke, making no effort to direct it away from Hannah's face.

She coughed, but kept her eyes on his face. "You must be devastated."

He shrugged. "Our good times were already in the past. Adele decided to move on. For all I know, she already had someone waiting in the wings."

"And you weren't upset about that?" Hannah tilted her head and waited for a reaction.

"Nope. There's plenty of fish in this sea." Moe glanced quickly at Karla.

Interesting, Hannah thought. What could be going on between *those* two? If anything.

"Your hometown boy isn't faring well, is he? The murder weapon found right next to Adele's body is an ominous sign for his immediate future."

"The way I see it, anyone could have taken that shovel. What were *you* doing this morning, so early on the beach?"

Moe shifted his weight from one foot to the other and took a drag on his unfiltered cigarette. "I like to watch the sunrise. And you?"

"What?" Hannah had a moment of panic. She had trouble sleeping the night before and did take an early morning stroll, but she hadn't seen Moe. Not even Cal knew she had gotten up and left their cozy sleepover with Olivia for a while. The only person she saw was her father returning to his cottage.

Moe laughed. "Be careful, Ms. Hannah Holiday. You might be biting off more than you can chew." Moe threw his cigarette butt on the ground and walked away.

Hannah seethed. She picked up the unsightly butt, wrapped it in a corner of a blank page ripped from her newly purchased book, and tucked it in her back pocket. She knew Moe's type. He thought he could get away with anything—including intimidation—but she'd show him how wrong he was.

"What was *that* all about?" Cal's comforting voice whispered in her ear. "And you even cleaned up his trash?"

"That Moe Meyer is up to something and I doubt it's any good. He was taunting me, pushing my buttons, trying to get under my skin." Hannah looked at Cal. "Why would he do that?"

"Maybe he senses you're a threat to him for some reason. Or else he just likes to be a jerk. I wonder why he doesn't leave town. Do you think he's been told to stick around? Could he be on the police's radar for Adele's murder, too? But that doesn't make sense if they're a couple."

"You know how you said he was dating Adele?"

Cal nodded. With his arm draped over Hannah's shoulder, they headed to the edge of the green.

"He told me they were done; Adele might have had someone waiting in the wings. And something else. I saw how he looked at Karla. I think he's hoping Rory gets locked away so he can move in on her. The guy is nothing but slime."

"Did you get any info from Karla while I had my sister distracted?"

Hannah slipped her phone from her pocket and checked the time. "She's meeting me at the marina in about a half hour when she's done helping with the book sale. I think she knows more than she realizes but it will take time for her to sort out all that has happened. At this point, she's pretty shell shocked."

"Monica knows Karla well from working with her at the library and she thinks Karla is holding something back, too. Monica said she overheard Rory and Karla arguing the day before the sand sculpting event."

"That could be about anything, though."

Cal took Hannah's hand and they dashed across the street. "It wasn't just anything. Karla gave Rory an ultimatum—if he didn't win the competition, she would leave him."

Hannah stopped, forcing Cal to pull her onto the sidewalk and away from the traffic. "So Rory lost something much more important than first place in the sculpting competition." Hannah glanced back toward the green. Could her father be right about Rory, or did someone else have plans to destroy his life?

CHAPTER 7

Cal and Hannah had enough time to walk from the marina along the beach that held the ruins of the sand sculptures. The crowds from the day before were long gone, replaced by seagulls and sandpipers. Hannah let her lungs take in the fresh salty breeze, her toes digging into the wet sand, and she squeezed Cal's fingers between her own. "What happened to Adele?" she asked, knowing Cal didn't have the answer.

"That's the million-dollar question, and it looks worse and worse for Rory."

They turned around and headed back the way they'd come. As they approached the marina, Hannah spotted Karla standing near the dock going out to Cal's boat. She had her phone to her ear and gestured dramatically.

"Time for a chit chat. Can we get comfy on your boat?" Hannah asked Cal.

"Sure. I've got some cold drinks and I might even be able to rustle up some snacks."

"Karla!" Hannah called and waved to get her attention. Karla turned away from Hannah and tucked her head down. She began walking away from the marina.

Hannah kicked her speed into overdrive. She angled her path toward the entrance to the marina, hoping to cut off Karla's route before she had time to disappear.

"What's your hurry?" Hannah asked as she pulled next to Karla.

"Oh. I just got a phone call. Can we talk another time?"

"No. I only need a few minutes of your time. We can have privacy on my friend's boat." Hannah pointed down the dock.

"Uh. How about my apartment? It's not far."

Hannah nodded. Anywhere would work, but she was surprised to hear that Karla had an apartment. She wasn't living with Rory?

They walked quickly. Hannah followed Karla up a set of stairs attached to the side of an old house on Main Street. She unlocked the door and waited for Hannah to follow her inside. "It's not really *my* apartment. It's Rory's, but he gave me a key."

Hannah nodded.

They stood in a small kitchen with the sink piled high with dirty dishes. Hannah could see a tiny living room beyond and a closed door off the living room.

"I know what you're thinking. This place isn't much. That's why I want to get out of here." Karla threw the keys on the table. She picked up a small dish but

Hannah saw that it was filled with cigarette butts before Karla dumped it in the sink.

Chills ran down Hannah's spine. Did Rory smoke or was Moe inside this apartment?

Karla twirled around and leaned against the sink. "So. What do you want to know?"

"You found Adele's body. What exactly did you see this morning?"

Karla tilted her head and sighed. She looked like she was resigned to sharing more than she wanted with Hannah and she started talking, "The mermaid sand sculpture was mostly washed away, but it must have been a barrier for the tide since Adele's body was away from the water. She looked like she was watching the sky or something, almost as if she lay down for a few minutes to rest. That was the weirdest part."

"It must have been a terrible shock for you."

"Yeah, pretty creepy. And then Moe showed up. He took my phone out of my hand and called 911. I turned into a statue but he functioned just fine. He waited with me until the police arrived, and he's the one who found the shovel. It almost seemed like he knew right where to look for it." A shiver ran through Karla's body.

"Did you go to the Pub and Pool Hall last night?" Hannah realized she changed the conversation's direction but she didn't know how long Karla would stand still to answer questions. She wanted to find out as much as possible about what Karla knew and where people were Friday night.

"What? That's an odd question."

"Is it?" Hannah pulled on her braid, trying to act casual.

"Sort of, but yeah, I was there, along with a pile of other people."

"It was the hang out after the competition?"

"You could say that." Karla snuck a peek at a text message on her phone. "Listen, I'm sort of busy."

A kitten, maybe eight or nine months old, wrapped his skinny body around Hannah's leg. She bent down, glad for the distraction. "Who's this cute little guy?"

Karla waved her hand. "That's Harvey. Rory's cat. He needs to find a home for him. We can't take him with us to Boston."

Hannah picked Harvey up and cradled him in her arms. "When are you leaving?"

Karla sighed. "I *said* I'm busy. *Enough* with the million and one questions." She moved toward the doorway to the living room and Hannah followed.

"Are these all Rory's sculptures?" Hannah's eyes moved around the room filled with sculptures made from old recycled materials. "They're fantastic. Has he tried to sell them? I'd be happy to find a place in my snack bar to display some." She balanced Harvey in the crook of one arm while she picked up a small metal lobster made from what looked like flattened tin cans.

Karla flicked her wrist. "Rory's problem is that he only cares about creating and can't..." She rolled her eyes and used her fingers to make air quotes. "'Lower himself to do any marketing'. How does he expect to make a living?"

The kitchen door opened. Karla's eyes darted around the room.

"Karla?"

Hannah recognized the voice but it made no sense. Until she remembered the dish filled with cigarette butts.

Moe stomped through the kitchen into the living room. "Well, fancy meeting Ms. Save-The-Beaches here. Not exactly who I was expecting. Are you ready to go, Karla?"

"Um, not yet. I haven't packed anything." She picked up a backpack from the couch and stuffed a sweatshirt inside. What will I need?"

"We're going to Florida, not the North Pole. Bring your bikini and some sandals."

Hannah couldn't believe her ears. She grabbed Karla's arm. "What about Rory? You're abandoning him when he needs you more than ever?"

"Rory's a loser. Karla finally saw the light." Moe leaned against the kitchen doorway, smoking. Ashes fell on the floor. He blew smoke rings. "Hurry up before that cranky police woman decides we can't leave town."

"I'm not sure, Moe. Hannah's right. Rory needs me." Her fingers stroked a pendant hanging around her neck. As she moved it back and forth, light reflected off it, catching Hannah's eye.

"Where did you get that?" Hannah asked.

"This?" Karla pulled the silver mermaid out as far as it would go and looked at it. "Moe gave it to me."

Hannah turned around, only to hear the kitchen door slam and Moe gone. She called Jack on the phone she hadn't even realized she'd pulled from her bag. "Call Pam, tell her to find Moe Meyer before he leaves town. She'll listen to you." Hannah looked at Karla. "What kind of car does Moe drive?"

Her eyes were wide saucers. "A Jeep Wrangler. Black."

Hannah gave Jack that information and hung up. "Sit down Karla. You have a lot more explaining to do."

Karla's face drained of color. She sat at the kitchen table. "What's with this necklace? Why did Moe run off after you asked about it?"

"When did Moe give it to you?"

"After we found Adele's body. He walked me back here, asked me to go to Florida with him, and gave me the necklace. He told me I was his mermaid."

Hannah leaned close to Karla. "Didn't that seem odd? You barely know him. And a mermaid? Like Adele's sand sculpture?"

She shrugged. "I guess so. Now it sounds strange, but at the time he made everything sound romantic and exciting." She looked at Hannah. "And possible. He said Rory was a dead end."

Hannah covered Karla's hand with her own. "What about last night—at the Pub and Pool Hall?"

"It was pretty wild. Adele was taunting Rory about her sculpture winning the competition, and Rory lost it. He usually doesn't pay attention to anything like that but she knew exactly how to push his buttons."

"What about Moe? He lost, too. Didn't it bother him?"

"Oh yeah. He was seething. Now I suspect that's probably why he started to flirt with me. To bug Rory *and* Adele." Karla dropped her head into her hands. "What did I get myself in the middle of?"

Hannah's phone rang. "Hi Jack." She listened to him go on and on about Pam looking for Moe, barely taking in his words. Finally, he paused for a moment and she said, "Okay, I'll bring her to the police station and meet you there."

Hannah stood. "Before we leave, where's the cat food? It looks like Harvey could use a fresh bowl of water and food."

"I have no idea where Rory kept it." She waved her hand around the small kitchen. "Look in the cupboards. I have to go to the bathroom."

It didn't take long to find half a bag of dry cat food but there wasn't a clean bowl anywhere. Hannah rinsed two small bowls, filling one with water and the other with dry food. "There you go, Harvey. I'll make sure you aren't forgotten here."

"Karla? Ready to go?" Hannah peered into the living room, not even sure which door led to the bathroom. She pushed one door open to find a bedroom that barely fit a twin bed. The only other door had to be the bathroom. Hannah knocked.

Silence.

She tried the doorknob. Locked. "Karla! Open up."

Hannah rattled the door.

She dashed from the apartment, down the stairs and around to the other side of the house. A small window was open where Hannah guessed the bathroom should be. She kicked a pile of leaves in frustration and called Jack.

"Karla's gone. She must have jumped out the bathroom window."

"Don't worry. Pam has Moe so Karla won't be leaving with him if that was her plan. What a mess. Go home if you want and I'll call when I have some information."

Hannah had to walk back to the green to find her car. She texted Cal on her way, careful not to walk into anything. *Going home*, she wrote.

One dead mermaid.

Two jealous boyfriends.

And three too many suspects.

Hannah couldn't wait to get to her new cottage and sit on the porch to let the ocean breeze blow away the problems swirling around.

She trudged up the path to *Slo N EZ*. Each step lightened her mood and left some worries behind. Nellie woofed from inside the cottage. Nellie, her best medicine.

Hannah opened the door, expecting her quiet sanctuary, but instead a voice surprised her.

"It's about time you got here."

Hannah held onto the door to keep from falling down.

In her wildest dream, this was the last person she ever expected to see.

CHAPTER 8

Great Aunt Caroline sat propped against a pile of sleeping bags under the pink tent in the middle of Hannah's living room.

Hannah closed her eyes and shook her head. Sure, she had a lot on her mind and she was overtired from barely sleeping the night before, but this had to be, what, a hallucination? A ghost?

"I know what you're thinking. Sit down here next to me and I'll catch you up to speed." Great Aunt Caroline patted a spot on Olivia's sleeping bag next to where she sat. "And for crying out loud, close the door before someone else sees me."

Hannah sat with Nellie's head in her lap. She touched her great aunt.

Caroline laughed. "Yes, honey, I'm as real as the sand outside your door. Sorry to show up like this, but drastic times mean drastic measures, and Jack said I had to help you out in person this time."

"But—"

Caroline patted Hannah's knee. "All you need to know is that I had to *die* in order to save you and my property from your father's plans. But with him here now, well, the danger is far too close for comfort."

"Who else knows?" Part of Hannah felt betrayed by the lie and whoever else was involved.

"About me? Jack, Pam, and Meg all worked together with me to come up with the plan. And old Doc Pratchet came out of retirement for one last important task of declaring me dead. We never expected it to go so smoothly, but, sometimes, life surprises us." She smiled at her great niece. "You can't imagine how wonderful it is to finally be able to sit here face-to-face with you. You're doing a fantastic job, you know. I'm incredibly proud of you."

Hannah's mouth opened but no sound came out. She focused on Nellie's soft fur under her fingers. Finally, she managed a question. "What was my father going to do?"

Caroline sighed. "Your father is a complicated man. Unfortunately, he always puts himself first and stops at nothing to fulfill his dreams. Do you remember the car accident you were in about six months before I 'died?'" She used her fingers for air quotes around her fake death.

Hannah nodded. "My brakes failed but I was barely scratched."

"I think it was a warning to me from your father to let me know what he was capable of. If he was willing to risk his own daughter's life to make a point, he would stop at nothing to take this piece of property from me."

Hannah's jaw fell to her chest. "No." How could she manage to wrap her head around the possibility of her father sabotaging her car's brakes?

"I don't have proof, but I wasn't willing to take a chance. If it meant giving up my life to save yours, it was a small price to pay." She shrugged. "Actually, it was by far the easiest decision of my life. I'm an old woman already, and being able to watch my death from the sidelines has been extremely interesting, to say the least."

Hannah wrapped her arms around herself to try to stop the internal shaking. Her own father? Could it be true?

Caroline stood but stayed well away from the window. "I can't stay here any longer. It's too risky." She pulled a shawl over her head and partly covered her face. "You had to hear what you are up against so anything out of the ordinary becomes a warning."

"Like Adele's death?" Hannah whispered.

"Yes. Treat that as part of your father's plan. I don't know how it fits in but I don't doubt he will use it to his advantage. He always does."

"How will you get out of here without being seen?"

"That's the least of my problems. Jack and Meg have a plan. And remember—" Caroline stared deep into Hannah's eyes as she held both of Hannah's hands in hers; the two sets of eyes so similar except for the many years that separated them. "I'm never far away. Jack can always get in touch with me if necessary. You need to leave now. Pam is having a little chat with your parents to keep them occupied and away from this cottage."

Caroline pushed Hannah toward the door. Nellie stood but stayed between the two women.

"Go on, Nellie." Caroline flicked her fingers toward Hannah. "You need to keep an eye on Hannah."

"You know Nellie?"

Caroline laughed. "I wanted you to have company and another set of eyes on your back. Jack did a good job convincing you to take her, didn't he? He has a lot of tricks up his old sleeves. And Hannah?"

Hannah turned around before she opened the door.

"Keep a very close eye on Olivia."

Hannah and Nellie left. She had a renewed sense of mission to find out the truth about Adele's death, but the warning about Olivia made her shudder. Maybe she should tell Ruby to leave with her until this was over. Did her father stop at nothing to get what he wanted?

She stumbled down the path, not at all sure of anything anymore. Who could she trust? Who could she depend on to help her? Was her life in danger? The last question seemed obvious if she believed anything Great Aunt Caroline told her. Her life must be in danger, but what direction would the threat come from?

"Are you okay?" Cal's concerned voice broke through her thoughts. "You look like you've seen a ghost."

If he only knew, Hannah thought.

He took her arm. "I came as soon as I could after I got your text message. What happened with Karla?"

Cal's questions brought Hannah totally back to Earth. "She was planning to run off to Florida with Moe. Can you believe it?"

"And?"

"Moe gave her Adele's mermaid necklace. When I pointed it out, Moe fled. Pam caught him, but Karla ran off too. I don't know where she is. So, the question is, how did Moe get the necklace?"

"You think *he's* the murderer?"

"At this point nothing is clear, but something happened at the Pub and Pool Hall last night that might clear everything up. Or get us one step closer. Rory, Moe, Karla, and Adele were all there. Adele won't be giving us any clues, but I think the other three all know more than they are saying."

"How about a bowl of chowder while we ponder the situation. I'm ravenous." Cal steered Hannah toward The Fishy Dish.

She glanced at the parking lot and was glad to see that Pam's cruiser was still parked front and center. She hoped that meant the coast was clear for Great Aunt Caroline to escape unnoticed.

"There goes Jack's truck," Cal pointed to the exit of The Fishy Dish parking lot. "Where's he off to in such a hurry?"

Hannah shrugged, but inside she let out a sigh of relief. Great Aunt Caroline must be with him and off to wherever she would be safely hidden. "I'll get the chowder. You grab us a couple of seats outside and iced tea from the cooler."

"Don't forget some extra packages of those oyster crackers. Please." Cal raised his eyebrows in a cute puppy dog manner which Hannah found to be completely irresistible.

Meg entered the back door of the kitchen at the same time Hannah walked in from the small seating area of The Fishy Dish. She put her hands on Hannah's shoulders. "Has your brain settled down yet?"

"I think so. I saw Jack's truck leave. Can I assume everything is all set?" Hannah asked. She searched Meg's face for any clues to what just happened.

"Almost. He still has to get through town." She smiled at Hannah. "I'm glad you finally know. That makes it a little easier for me and Jack now." She kept her eyes on Hannah for a few more seconds before she moved away. She tied an apron around her waist and pulled a large bowl of coleslaw from the refrigerator. "Back to work. One good thing about a murder in town is that business picks up."

And plenty of unexpected surprises, Hannah said to herself. She filled two bowls with Meg's clam chowder and heaped a pile of oyster cracker packets on a tray next to the bowls.

"Speaking about the murder, do you want to make a trip to your brother's Pub and Pool Hall with me after work? From what Karla Vaughn told me, it sounds like that's where all the problems started last night. Maybe Michael can give us some more details about what happened."

"That's interesting. Michael already called me and said to swing by for some beer and chit chat—his code for, you definitely want to hear what I know. I'll pick you up at seven?"

"I can drive." Hannah hated Meg's truck but she didn't want to insult her.

Meg put her hands on her hips. "No thanks. You can suck it up for one night and ride with me." The edge of her mouth twitched a little. "Me, my truck, and my brother, or no deal."

Hannah rolled her eyes. "You win. I'll be ready at seven."

She picked up her tray and hurried through the door to find Cal. Of course, her expectation for a quiet and relaxing bite to eat crumbled like a delicate sand castle when she saw her father sitting next to Cal.

Luke's finger stabbed repeatedly toward the parking lot. As she moved closer, she could see a vein pulsing on his forehead and his nostrils flared.

It was now or never to get some details from his interaction with Adele.

Hannah moved to the far side of the picnic table from her father even though she preferred to face the ocean.

Luke helped himself to one of the bowls of chowder before Hannah could claim it. Oh well; with her stomach in knots, food was not at the top of her needs.

Cal pushed the second bowl toward Hannah. "You take this one and stay here with your father. I can take care of myself."

Hannah smiled at Cal but forced her face to keep the smile for her father, too. If she hoped to make any progress with him, it wouldn't serve her well to put him on the defensive. Stroking his ego just might get him to let his guard down a smidge.

"Where's Mom?" Hannah asked, hoping that was a safe subject to begin their conversation with.

"You know how Joanna is. With all the drama surrounding Adele, and that horrid police woman grilling us like we had something to do with her death, your mother is laid up with one of her bloody migraines. I doubt she'll leave that stinking cottage for the rest of our visit."

Hannah bit her tongue. Her father was waiting for her to take the bait after he insulted *Something's Fishy*. "There are other places to stay in town if you aren't comfortable in my cozy cottage. The Paradise Inn is more centrally located. Maybe that would suit you better?" she calmly suggested.

Luke waved his hand. "No, we want to be close to you." He sipped the chowder and made a face. "This is much too salty." He pushed the bowl away. "Haven't you played long enough at this business thing, Hannah?"

She crossed her legs and took several big spoonful's of the chowder to give herself time to control the pace of the conversation. Control was everything with Luke, and Hannah made a calculated decision to take control out of his hand. "Actually, this chowder wins every competition we enter. Maybe clam chowder just doesn't work with your taste buds. Have you considered that?"

Luke softened his approach. "I understand that you love this ocean view, but wouldn't it be better to build a big hotel here so more people could enjoy it, too? And you'd make so much more money. Your mother and I think you work much too hard."

Hannah hated it when he brought her mother into the conversation when she wasn't there. Did he think two against one would be more persuasive? "The way I look at it is that it isn't really work when you love what you are doing."

Luke slammed his hand on the table. "You've always done the exact opposite of what is in your best interest. This is all Caroline's fault. Even with her dead and buried, she still seems to be controlling you." He stood and almost fell when the heel of his shoe caught on the picnic table bench as he lifted his leg over. "Have it your way, Hannah, but you're heading down a difficult path and I have no intention of bailing you out when this," he swept his arm in a one hundred and eighty degree arc, "comes crashing down around you."

Hannah stood, too, she would rather be close to his eye level rather than having him tower over her while she sat. "I don't want—or expect—you to *ever* bail me out. All I've ever wanted from you was for you to accept me for who I am, but apparently that's impossible. You always hoped Ruby and I would be more like Adele: a shallow, conniving, liar." She turned and walked back toward The Fishy Dish before she said something she might *really* regret.

She wasn't quick enough to avoid his stabbing words. "You will wish you never set foot on this piece of sand."

CHAPTER 9

"Did he just threaten you?" Cal asked when Hannah reached the safety of the counter where he had been watching the interaction. His hands were clenched and he took several steps in Luke's direction.

Hannah pulled on his arm. "Nothing I haven't heard for many years. The difference now is that I refuse to feel even the tiniest bit of guilt for disappointing him. Now I see it as a badge of courage to finally be able to stand up to his bullying."

"What changed?"

It dawned on Hannah that when Great Aunt Caroline came back into her life, appreciating her for who she was, it gave her a strength she didn't know she had. "I see who he is and not what I hoped he would be." She desperately wanted to tell Cal about Great Aunt Caroline, but the less people who knew, the better. She wouldn't even tell Ruby.

"What are you going to do about him?"

Hannah shrugged. "Try to ignore him? Run my life exactly how I need to. Try to help Rory any way I can. Try to keep Karla from making the biggest mistake of her life by following Moe to Florida. And keep my fingers crossed that nothing else terrible happens between now and when my parents leave." She probably should have left that last comment unsaid since Cal gave her a quizzical look.

"Reading between the lines, it sounds like you will be on guard until they leave. What's going on? I don't want to be worrying about you every minute you're out of my sight."

"My father hates it if anyone stands up to him and I've done it to varying degrees since I was a teenager." She chose her words carefully. "What you just heard me tell him about Adele was putting words to her actions, and the truth hurts. He can't admit he was wrong in his admiration for a person who he constantly held up as someone he thought should be a role model for me and Ruby." Hannah felt tears threaten to spill over the rims of her eyes. Why did she still care what that man thought? She swiped the wetness away. She cared because, no matter what, he *was* her father. The only one she'd ever get.

Cal pulled her close. "What a fool he is, but you know what?"

Hannah sniffled.

"When Caroline left this property to you, she also left you with people who believe in you and see your strength and goodness, even if your own father can't see beyond that wart on the end of his nose."

Hannah pulled away to be able to look into Cal's face. "He doesn't have a wart."

Cal smiled at her. "I know."

They both laughed, and just like that, Hannah knew Cal hit the heart of Great Aunt Caroline's gift to her— friends that would never let her down and would make her laugh when what she really wanted to do was crawl inside Olivia's pink tent and hide from the world.

Olivia.

She had to take Great Aunt Caroline's warning seriously. But, at the same time, she couldn't expect Ruby to up and leave town, pulling Olivia out of school, without revealing the fact that Great Aunt Caroline was really alive. She would have to be smart and watchful with Meg and Jack's help. And Nellie. And she couldn't forget about Pam. *She* knew the truth, too. Maybe this could be common ground for the beginning of a friendship.

"I've got the answer to all your problems." Cal's eyes twinkled. "A prescription that works every time."

Hannah couldn't help but feel better with the anticipation of what he might be offering. He led her to one of the picnic tables and had her sit facing the ocean. "I'll be back in less time than it takes for a few waves to crash on the beach."

The surf crashed, kids screeched happily, and the seafood aroma wafting from The Fishy Dish all melded together to sooth Hannah.

"Close your eyes," Cal's rich voice sounded just behind her. She felt his thigh against her back. She closed her eyes.

"Open your mouth."

She did as ordered.

A giant spoonful of cold, creamy, sweet vanilla ice cream with hot fudge sauce landed on her tongue. Cal plunked down on the picnic table bench next to her. "Here you go. I'm not feeding you the rest; you can do it yourself."

Hannah took the cup filled with a hot fudge sundae and offered a spoonful to Cal.

"Okay, if you insist." He took the ice cream and held the spoon between his teeth.

"Hey! Give it back so I can have a bite."

They leaned against each other and shared the ice cream. "This is your prescription, Dr. Murphy?"

"Sometimes it takes drastic measures to melt away a funky mood. Is it working?"

"Uh-huh," Hannah mumbled through a mouthful of cold deliciousness. "Sure is!"

"Now that you're smiling, I can leave for the marina. I have some dock repairs to finish today. Do you think you can live without me for a few hours?"

"I don't know about that." Hannah bumped her shoulder into Cal.

"The more important question is: Can you stay out of trouble?"

"That's my plan." But Hannah knew that plans didn't always go as intended. Her first order of business would be to talk to Deputy Pam Larson to be sure Olivia was safe and possibly find some common ground in their relationship. And, of course, her visit with Meg to the Pub and Pool Hall would tie up her evening.

After Cal left, Hannah stepped up to help during the busy lunch time. Fried fish platters, heaping with hand-cut fries, lobster rolls, and steaming clam chowder flew from the kitchen as fast as Hannah and Samantha could deliver them. Ruby dished out ice cream without a break while Olivia sat at the counter with her coloring book.

While Hannah returned to the kitchen for a large order of Meg's hand-cut French fries and fish sandwiches for a rowdy group of tourists, Meg signaled for her to check on her niece. "Get out there, Hannah. Quick!"

Hannah shoved her tray of fries and fish sandwiches into Samantha's arms and rushed to the counter next to the ice cream window.

"And this is my favorite color, pink," Olivia explained to her grandfather.

"I could take you to the store so you could—"

Hannah pushed in between her father and her niece. "I don't think so, Dad. Olivia and I already have plans. Besides," she turned to face Luke, "did you even think to ask Ruby first before you barge in and make a bunch of promises?"

Luke held his hands up. "Wow, since when did you become the protective mama bear around here? Ruby's working and I thought it might help her out if I spent some time with Olivia. Besides, I've barely had any time with my granddaughter yet."

"Yeah, well, she's not going with you." Hannah kept her body between Luke and Olivia. She knew it probably sounded ridiculous to anyone else, but after Great Aunt Caroline's warning, there was no way Luke would have any alone time with Olivia.

"Hannah's right, Dad. Olivia doesn't know you at all. She was only four the last time you visited us." Ruby stood shoulder-to-shoulder with Hannah.

"Fine. No loss to me. It's your kid who would have benefited from my shopping spree."

"Stuff isn't what kids need. But, of course, that was always your solution to a guilty conscience—throw a gift our way. You know what happened to all those gifts?"

Luke's jaw tightened and his face turned an ugly shade of purple.

"We threw every single one away. You didn't know our favorite color, or our favorite food. You bought stuff you decided was good for us but it was never anything we wanted."

Hannah's eyes stared straight into her father's. She refused to turn away first.

Luke smoldered. "You act exactly like Caroline. No concern for anyone else's feelings or even for your own best interest. But, don't worry, I promised your mother we wouldn't leave until we get you to see the benefit of selling this business that is only a weight around your neck. Sell it before it drowns you."

"There is nothing that will make me sell." Hannah spit the words at her father.

Luke laughed. "Oh, I wouldn't be so sure of that." He patted Olivia's head before he walked to the parking lot and drove away.

Hannah's legs began to tremble. She held onto the counter to keep from falling. Anger replaced her fear. What was he planning to do?

"Hannah?" Ruby gently pulled her sister out of hearing range of Olivia. "What is going on? I never saw you and Dad get into such a war of words."

"You heard him, Ruby. He wants me to sell all this so I can use the money to travel. He's deciding, like always, what he thinks is best for me and I'm not going to let him bully me." Hannah stared at her sister. Would Ruby back her up?

"Of course you can't sell. You love it here. Olivia and I love it here. Why does Dad care?"

"I'm not sure," Hannah lied. She knew exactly why, and it was revenge against Great Aunt Caroline for leaving the property to her instead of to him. But she couldn't tell Ruby that. Not yet, at least.

"What are you going to do?"

"It looks like the lunch hour rush has died down so I'm going to the police station and find out what's going on with Rory. Dad came to town because he wanted to see Adele. She's dead and I think Dad is going to do everything he can to make sure Rory is arrested and thrown into jail for her murder. I don't know how that's connected to this property, but I have a sinking feeling that I will find out sooner or later."

"Maybe Jack can get that information for you from his daughter. You and Pam don't have the closest of relationships."

"I'll definitely talk to Jack first." Hannah couldn't tell Ruby that her other motive for talking to Pam was to be sure the police kept an eye on her father with the hope of keeping Olivia safe.

CHAPTER 10

When Hannah arrived at Jack's house, she saw him through the living room window sitting in his comfy chair. She opened the door.

"Jack? Can I come in?"

"Sounds like you're already in so why are you asking? And you're probably expecting some coffee, too."

Hannah chuckled. Jack certainly liked to sound tough. "You read my mind. Coffee sounds perfect. Thanks for the offer." Jack's coffee was strong, black, and rich. Exactly how she liked it.

She made herself comfortable at his kitchen table while he busied himself with his coffee machine. He spilled some grounds on the counter when he measured, the water splashed over the edge of the container, and he mumbled something about drop-in guests being a pain in the neck.

Hannah heard him and knew it was all a big act. He most likely was letting off steam from the stress of transporting Great Aunt Caroline.

"I'm glad you finally know about Caroline. It was killing me to keep that secret. Meg, too," he finally admitted to Hannah.

Hannah gave herself a mental pat on the back. She called that right. "Yeah, Meg said the same thing."

He turned around and looked at Hannah. "Are you okay? Caroline said you acted like you thought she was a ghost. You even had to touch her to be sure she was real." His lips curled at the edges and grew into a big grin. "I wish I could have been there to see it with my own old eyes."

"I'm not sure about the okay part, to be honest. I have to figure out what my father's up to, watch over Olivia like a hawk, and keep Rory out of jail. How am I supposed to do all that?" Hannah rested her chin in her upturned palms, her elbows squarely on the table.

"I'm going to help with the Olivia part while you and Meg go to the Pub and Pool Hall. Whatever your father is up to will reveal itself in its own time." He poured coffee into two mugs even though he set three on the table. "By the way, what did you tell Cal? He must have suspected something was wrong when he saw you after you left Caroline."

"I didn't tell him anything. We talked about Karla and Moe." She sighed deeply and shook her head. "I don't know how you kept Great Aunt Caroline's 'death' a secret. I hope I don't slip up."

"We came close to slipping up plenty of times but, really, who would believe it without seeing her with their own eyes? Everyone thinks she's dead. You'll be fine. Just try to forget about it for now and focus on the here and now."

"You mean, murder and who done it?"

Jack chuckled. "Exactly."

Hannah clinked her mug against the empty one. "Expecting someone else?"

"Uh-huh. Any minute." Jack sat across from Hannah. Apparently, he loved secrets and had no intention of giving Hannah any more information about the mystery guest. "About your father. Have you asked him where he was after he had dinner with Adele?"

Hannah shook her head.

"He went to the Pub and Pool Hall, too. It doesn't seem like his sort of place with his world traveling, better-than-everyone-else attitude."

"Did my mother go with him?"

"Nope. I haven't heard what she did; maybe she decided to have any early night in the cottage. Read a book or something."

"That sounds like her."

Footsteps sounded in Jack's living room. Obviously, his guest felt at home coming right in.

"I smell coffee, hope it's still hot."

Hannah knew the voice. It probably wasn't a coincidence that Jack's daughter, Pam, arrived while Hannah was visiting. It was just like Jack to throw them together with the hope that Pam, being a Hooks Harbor police deputy, might shed some light on Adele's murder. Not that Pam was usually very helpful, as far as Hannah was concerned.

"For the ghost whisperer," Pam said as she plopped a pastry box on the table. "I couldn't resist picking up some orange frosted chocolate cupcakes from Simply Sweets." She sat in the third chair and adjusted her glasses higher on her nose.

Hannah snorted. She didn't know Pam had a shred of a sense of humor. She lifted the lid of the box and helped herself. "To my latest career path." She slid the box toward Jack so he could help himself, too.

Jack filled the third mug for Pam and topped off Hannah's mug with the last of the coffee. "I heard it was a real spooky time," Jack added. "Poor Hannah almost wet herself."

Hannah tried to slap Jack's arm but he dodged just in time. "That's just mean, Jack. I almost fainted, but I was never even close to wetting myself." She bit into the cupcake and tried to sound annoyed. "Glad you two are so entertained by my shock of a lifetime."

Pam pulled the paper off a cupcake. "Wouldn't it be great if Caroline put on her white gauzy dress and walked the beach during a full moon? I can think of more than a few people who might have a heart attack if she appeared like that."

"Really, Pam? Aren't you an officer of the law? And here you are hoping for people to have heart attacks? I am shocked!" Hannah put her hand over her heart.

"Okay, you two, that's enough sarcasm. Now that we're here together, we need to make a plan. Caroline said Olivia might be in danger. Luke is brewing up something to steal Hannah's ocean front property. And, at the same time, someone has to figure out who killed Adele Bailey." Jack looked directly at his daughter. "Are you making any progress on that last problem, Pam?"

"You know I can't tell you that Rory's alibi is about as elusive as Caroline, or Karla had a lover's spat with him. But I can tell you that Moe tried to leave town, since Hannah's the one that tipped us off about his plans in the first place." She glanced at Hannah. "Thanks for that."

Who was this new Deputy Pam Larson who was treating Hannah like a normal person?

"I see a shocked expression on your face," Pam said to Hannah. "Caroline told me to cut you some slack, so don't let me down. And don't get in my way. Understand?"

"Ah, sure. Don't we want the same thing? To find out who murdered Adele Bailey? The way I see it, Rory,

Moe, and Karla all have motives to varying degrees and, possibly, they all had opportunity. I think I can get close to them and find out more information than they'd be willing to share with you. Is that a problem?"

Pam pulled her glasses off and chewed on the arm. "There's no law against you talking to whoever you want to, but be careful. I don't want to end up investigating who killed Hannah Holiday. That's my biggest concern when you start to poke around and stir up a hornet's nest."

Hannah licked the chocolate crumbs from the edge of her mouth and slid her chair back. "Fair enough. Oh, I almost forgot. When I was with Karla, she had a mermaid necklace she said Moe gave to her. I'm pretty sure it belonged to Adele."

"Moe explained that Adele returned it to him when she ended their relationship."

"Moe gave Karla a returned gift from a different girlfriend? Real classy," Jack said, his eyes rolling so far into his head they could have fallen out.

"I was thinking he took it from Adele after he slammed her in the back of her head with Rory's shovel. That would have tied him to her pretty easily," Hannah suggested, thinking it sounded like a more than plausible scenario.

"Moe isn't that stupid," Pam said. "He almost slipped out of town but, until we check out his alibi, I told him to stay put."

"He has an alibi?" Hannah asked.

Pam tilted her head. "Yeah. He said he saw you on the beach near the marina. Did you see him?"

Hannah's heart flip flopped. "No. I had trouble sleeping and walked along my stretch of beach, but I wasn't near the beach with the sand sculptures. What was he up to?"

"He said he was walking off all the stress of the competition. One more question," Pam said. "What time did your father get back to the cottage?" She flipped some pages in her notebook. "He told me he was back around midnight?"

Hannah shrugged. "If he got back then, he went out again because I saw him when I was out around fourish. I haven't spent much time with him, but I can try to find out more details from my mom. She's a bit easier to have an actual conversation with and not come away feeling like a tidal wave crashed over me."

Pam nodded. "He wasn't particularly cooperative when I questioned him this morning. Very evasive and answered with riddles in many cases. What's he hiding?"

"It's how he controls the situation. He's a master," Hannah answered. "My plan is to get under his skin to throw him off balance instead of letting him needle me."

"Good luck with that," Jack said. "Caroline warned me about your father but she has complete confidence in your ability to outsmart him."

"Let's hope so." Hannah grabbed another cupcake before she left Jack's house to search through Great Aunt Caroline's old trunk in case something important was hiding in plain sight; something that even Caroline had forgotten about.

CHAPTER 11

Hannah slid the heavy trunk out of her closet. She needed to lug it to her new cottage anyway, so with an old blanket covering it, she pulled it up the hill to *Slo N EZ*. Sitting on the floor with her legs crossed and her back against the wall, she lifted the lid.

Most of the items were old clothes that Hannah didn't want to donate, and some of Caroline's personal items including jewelry, knick knacks, and even an old doll. What Hannah dug underneath everything else for was a bundle of letters tied together with a purple ribbon. It seemed too personal to read when she first moved in, but under the current circumstances, she decided to take a look.

Not knowing what to expect, what she found surprised her thoroughly. The bulk of the letters were from Hannah's mother. How strange that Joanna would keep in touch with Great Aunt Caroline when her father forbade any correspondence.

One letter after the other chronicled Hannah's and Ruby's lives in California. Nothing out of the ordinary, but Joanna shared school and sporting events, and even snippets about Luke with Great Aunt Caroline. It was interesting and unexpected in more ways than one. Hannah never knew her mother to disagree with her father or go against his wishes. Joanna moved up a notch on Hannah's admiration chart.

Footsteps sounding on the porch outside startled Hannah. She quickly shoved the letters to the bottom of the trunk. She barely got the trunk covered with the old blanket before she saw her mother's face through the window in the door.

Guilt filled her gut. Hannah should have checked to see how her mother was feeling after her father left.

"Mom. You found me," Hannah said as she pulled the door open. "Not that I was hiding," she added, hoping her words didn't convey the guilt she felt. She'd never told them she was staying in *Slo N EZ*.

"Jack was in the office and suggested I check up here. This is your new cottage?" Joanna looked around Hannah into the cottage.

"Yeah, come on in. I haven't finished moving in yet, as you can tell." Hannah stepped aside and held her arm out for her mother to enter.

"Nice pink tent. You always did have a fondness for sleeping on the floor," Joanna teased.

"I made this for Olivia. We had a sleepover here last night. Let's sit on the porch and enjoy the view."

"And the chairs." Joanna laughed.

"And that. Is your migraine gone?"

"I think so. Your father was kind enough to entertain himself so I could sleep for most of the day." Joanna put her hand on Hannah's arm. "He's worried about you, you know."

Hannah clenched her jaw. "I don't think he's worried about me. He thinks he knows what's best for me and I don't agree. Let's leave it at that."

Joanna sighed. "I won't interfere. We missed you and Ruby at dinner last night."

That sentiment made it easy for Hannah to jump into the subject of Adele and get some information out of her mother. "How *was* your dinner with Adele last night? She must have been excited to win the competition."

Joanna smiled. "Adele was, I don't know, distracted. She kept getting text messages which annoyed your father. You know how he expects to have your undivided attention during a meal. Anyway, there was definitely something bothering her but she tried to cover it up with laughing and chatting, but it didn't fool me."

"What did she do after dinner? Did she meet anyone?"

Joanna ran her fingers through her hair. "She said she was going to play pool somewhere. I didn't pay too much attention since I was tired and wanted to go back to the cottage to read and relax. Your father gave her a ride after he dropped me off. He must have stayed and had a beer or two because I never even heard him come back."

Most likely, Hannah's father gave Adele a ride so he could keep an eye on her. Having a beer at the Pub and Pool Hall was definitely *not* Luke Holiday's cup of tea, but he could lower himself if it gave him an excuse to watch over his cherished Adele.

"Did Dad say anything to you about who Adele was with?"

"As soon as we heard the news about Adele, he mentioned that boy who came in second in the sand sculpting competition. He and Adele argued. Your father said everyone witnessed it. I don't know, Hannah. When your father makes up his mind about something, he never lets go."

Hannah wasn't going to disagree with that statement. Luke would do everything in his power to send Rory to prison if that was his goal. He also would continue to work on Hannah to sell her property. The question was, what angle would he come from? He'd already tried the direct approach and gotten nowhere. "How long are you and Dad staying in Hooks Harbor?"

Joanna flipped both hands up and shrugged. "That police woman told us to stick around so I guess we have to stay until Adele's murder is solved."

"You and Dad are suspects?" Hannah's voice rose in shock.

"She never actually used that word, but since your dad was one of the last people to see her alive, she has to check alibis and that sort of thing, I guess. It doesn't really matter since your dad doesn't seem to be in any sort of rush to get going."

"And you?"

"Except for visiting with you, Ruby, and Olivia, I would love to put this whole mess behind me."

Joanna hated conflict and drama but Luke thrived on it. Hannah's parents were definitely the opposites-attract type of a couple. To be honest, Hannah never could understand how her mother could tolerate her father but she chose to accept it for her mother's sake.

Hannah patted her mother's leg. "I'm sure Dad will get bored here sooner rather than later."

"I don't know about that. You know I try not to get between you and your father, but..."

Hannah's stomach twisted in a knot. Any statement from Joanna that started with her bringing up getting between Hannah and her dad couldn't be going anywhere good.

After a long pause, Joanna continued. "He's dead set on you selling this property. I think it's some kind of last revenge against Caroline since he always expected to inherit it." Joanna stood. "Be careful, honey."

Hannah leapt to her feet and grabbed her mother's arm. "Be careful? Is Dad going to hurt me?"

"Oh no, nothing like that. But I don't doubt that he has a plan that will make you choose between your property and something else that's even more important to you. I had to warn you."

And just like that, Joanna walked away from the cottage, her head down, her feet shuffling like an old, defeated person.

Hannah watched her mother walk to the beach and disappear. What could her father be planning? No point in making wild guesses. She locked the door of her new cottage and returned to Cottage One.

As Hannah reached for the door, it burst open.

"Samantha? What are you doing in here?" Hannah's hand flew to her chest.

Of course, Samantha wanted to know everything about what was going on connected to Adele's murder. She fancied herself a private investigator, at least that had always been her dream and she always managed to get involved in the nitty gritty details surrounding anything interesting.

Samantha grabbed Hannah's hand and pulled her inside. For a petite eighty-year-old, she had plenty of strength in her grip. "Your dad has been stirring up trouble."

Hannah followed Samantha inside and slammed the door shut. Hopefully, there wouldn't be any more interruptions. She opened her refrigerator, hoping to find something quick to eat while Samantha chattered in the background. Hannah twirled around when she heard Samantha mention her niece's name.

"What did you say about Olivia?"

"Luke wants to take her to the aquarium in Boston. He didn't even ask Ruby before he brainwashed Olivia, and now Ruby's in an uproar. You have to fix this."

"That man is nothing but trouble. Great Aunt Caroline warned me about this."

Samantha cocked her head. "When did she warn you?"

Oops. Hannah gave herself a mental slap on the side of her head. "A letter. In a letter I found in her trunk. Um, Great Aunt Caroline said to keep an eye on Olivia."

"And she mentioned Luke in the letter, too? That seems odd."

"I'm jumping to conclusions. You know, keep an eye on Olivia and now something has come up." Hannah watched Samantha's reaction carefully, and just like Jack predicted, what else could Samantha do but accept Hannah's explanation? Why would anyone suspect Great Aunt Caroline could still be alive?

"Your great aunt certainly had some foresight. What other advice did she give you?"

"That my father always expected to inherit this property and he would stop at nothing to get it." Why not give Samantha that tidbit? It wouldn't hurt to have an extra pair of eyes watching Luke *and* Olivia.

"Harrumph. That's not going to happen. Your father must think pretty highly of himself."

Hannah chuckled. "He sure does. You could teach him a thing or two."

A grin spread across Samantha's face. "I love a challenge, my dear, and you've just given me my next project—teach Mr. Luke Holiday that sometimes life gets swept off course by a riptide."

CHAPTER 12

Meg showed up in the Fishy Dish parking lot exactly at seven. With her truck popping, rattling, and backfiring, no one could miss her arrival even if their head was buried in the sand *and* they were hard of hearing.

Hannah grimaced. She hated riding in Meg's truck. She always worried that they might never arrive at their destination. At least, not without having to walk the last few miles.

Samantha jumped up and tried to kick her heels together. It didn't work. Hannah caught her before she crashed.

"This is so exciting," Samantha said. "I hate to complain, but life was getting kind of boring around here." She ticked off her agenda on her fingers. "Make coleslaw. Feed hungry people. Clean up. Start all over again. A dose of excitement is exactly what I need."

Hannah listened and found nothing wrong with Samantha's description of how the days went by at The Fishy Dish. Especially in comparison to the problems crashing around her at the moment. She'd take a nice boring routine over worrying about who killed Adele, what her father was planning, and keeping Olivia out of danger. She stuffed some bills in the pocket of her jeans and held the door for Samantha.

"Take care of everything while I'm gone, Nellie."

Nellie raised her head off the couch and woofed.

Right, Hannah thought. If anyone broke in with a juicy bone for Nellie, they'd be able to clean the place out. The only satisfaction with that thought was that there was nothing of value. As a matter of fact, it would simplify her life and save Hannah from carting the rest of her belongings from this cottage to the new one.

Meg beeped the horn of her truck and stuck her head out the window. "Let's move it, you two. We've got places to go and things to do."

Wow, both Meg and Samantha acted like all the drama surrounding Adele's death was an excuse to have a good time. All Hannah felt was dread and despair. Of course, they didn't have the worry of losing a business or keeping their eye on a six-year-old to weigh them down.

"Why the long face?" Meg asked Hannah as she climbed into the back bench seat of the truck, leaving the front death trap for Samantha.

"Sorry if I'm not as enthusiastic as you two are to be out looking for a murderer."

Meg and Samantha exchanged a look and shrugged their shoulders.

"I think you're looking at this all wrong, Hannah," Meg began. "We're trying to put a puzzle together, one piece at a time. If all the pieces fit, then we'll have the murderer. Why not have some fun before we get to that last piece? Play some pool, drink a few beers, ask a few questions, and maybe even flirt a little at the Pub and Pool Hall." She twitched one eyebrow up and down.

"You two can do the flirting."

"Unless Cal is there," Samantha teased.

That produced a small lip spasm from Hannah. "Yeah, unless Cal is there." She hoped he didn't show up though, since he would be a major distraction from her goal of observing and eavesdropping. Tonight felt more like a job than a night out and she wanted it to be as productive as possible instead of looking into his ocean blue eyes and dreaming of rocking to sleep on his boat.

After half-listening to Meg and Samantha chatter about some of the tourists who'd showed up at The Fishy Dish, Meg's truck bounced over the potholes in the parking lot of the Pub and Pool Hall.

"Ouch." Hannah pushed herself forward so she was barely balanced at the edge of the seat.

Meg chortled. "You must have found the broken spring with that last pothole I hit."

"I think it poked a hole through my jeans."

"I hope there isn't any blood on my backseat." Meg twisted her head around to look at Hannah.

"No worries in that department, just a chunk of denim. Hey." Hannah pointed to the Pub and Pool Hall sign on the roof of the building. "Your brother fixed the lights. I think I prefer the uniqueness of *ub and Poo all*."

"Don't worry, someone will have too much to drink, climb on the roof, and restore the sign to its infamous nature," Meg said. "It's impossible for Michael to keep up with his customers' pranks, but he did install a security camera to try to scare away the scoundrels."

Hannah waited for Samantha to get out so she could squeeze around the front seat. She straightened, twisted from one side to the other, and felt her back pop.

"Don't say anything about riding in the back or you'll be walking home," Meg warned.

Hannah bit her tongue but she wondered if walking might be preferable to a return trip in Meg's rust bucket. She'd make that decision when it was time to leave.

"Looks like a medium crowd for a Saturday night," Meg said as she led the way to the door and opened it. "Age before beauty," she said to Samantha.

"Darn tootin', my dear." Samantha sashayed inside as if she owned the place. She primped her hair and scanned the pool hall looking for her prey like a cheetah on the prowl.

Meg linked her arm through Hannah's. "Lighten up and enjoy yourself. I know you're still trying to sort out all this murder stuff plus deal with, you know, your mystery guest," she whispered conspiratorially, "but try to relax and go with the flow."

Hannah nodded. "Good advice. Let's get a couple of beers and see where the night brings us."

Meg slapped Hannah on her back. "Now you're talking. Hey, Michael, two Sam Adams for your two favorite girls."

"What about Samantha?" Michael asked.

"She can take care of herself."

Meg slid onto a barstool near the quiet end of the room and Hannah sat next to her.

"How are you, Hannah? You haven't honored me with your presence for a while. But I'll forgive you." Michael expertly slid two beers down the glossy bar. One stopped in front of Meg and the other in front of Hannah. He beamed with pride. "That trick took me years of practice to perfect."

Hannah sipped her beer before she casually scanned the room. She was shocked to see Moe and Karla at the pool table. Moe had the happy face of someone who'd downed a few too many beers, but Karla looked like she'd rather be anywhere else. Florida, or with Rory for starters.

Meg jabbed Hannah with her elbow, almost causing a big spill.

"What's that for?" Hannah moved her arm away from another potential attack.

"Look who Samantha's talking to." Meg nodded her head toward the far corner of the hall. "And don't stare."

Hannah twirled her barstool partway around so she was mostly facing Meg but could see the rest of the hall from the corner of her eye. What met her eye made her choke on her mouthful of beer. She hissed, "My father? What's he doing here?"

"The bigger question is, what the heck is Samantha doing? Is she flirting with him?"

Michael reached under the bar and gave Meg a small mirror. "Use this if you want to see what's going on."

"Clever, brother," Meg said. "She took the mirror and pretended to check her nonexistent makeup. "Can I ask you a question about your parents?"

"Sure," Hannah answered.

"Is their marriage solid?" Meg's eyebrows shot up as she waited for Hannah's reply.

Hannah shrugged. "As far as I know." She leaned close to Meg to look in the mirror. Her hand covered her mouth but a snort snuck out. "Samantha is doing a number on my dad. Ewww. Really? Don't touch his hair," Hannah said as if Samantha could hear her.

Meg lowered the mirror. "Do you think Samantha has lost her mind? She *does* know who she's flirting with, doesn't she?"

Hannah drained half of her beer. "She's hoping to teach him a lesson about life."

"That should be interesting." Meg chuckled.

"Yeah, teach him that he can't always get his way." Hannah slid off the barstool. "Let's see if we can break into that game of pool."

Meg hip-checked Hannah. "Glad you've got your game face on finally." They walked toward the pool table. "Hey, ready for a little competition?"

Moe looked up and grinned at Hannah. "Always."

Karla's eyes darted between Moe and Hannah. "I'm getting a beer."

"Great," Meg said. "It's you and me then, big boy." Meg slapped Moe on the back. "My friend can keep your friend company."

Karla was already at the bar waiting for her beer by the time Hannah sat next to her. "I'll have another Sam Adams, Michael."

"Don't tell me *I told you so*," Karla mumbled more to her beer than to Hannah. "Moe's a jerk."

"Why are you here with him then?"

"I'm not here *with* him. I'm searching for answers. Rory hasn't been charged yet but the police have him locked up. What's up with that?"

"He can be held for forty eight hours without any charge but he needs a lawyer. A good one," Hannah said as gently as possible.

"Right. He has no money for a lawyer, good or bad."

Hannah covered Karla's hand with her own. "I'll help but you need to tell me everything."

"I don't know who killed Adele."

"Maybe not, but you must have seen or heard something that could lead the police to the killer."

Karla swiveled the barstool to face Hannah. "Like what?"

"Okay, let's start with the award ceremony Friday night and then try to remember everything that happened here at the Pub and Pool Hall up until Adele left. Who was she talking to? Who did she leave with? Any detail you can think of."

"The award ceremony is a blur, but plenty happened here Friday night. Adele put herself in the center of everything. She was pretty drunk and that guy," Karla nodded toward Hannah's father, "he kept trying to get her to leave with him. I'm not sure what that was about, but Adele finally yelled at him and told him to leave her alone. He got mad at her."

Hannah glanced at her father and Samantha. Luke sat nursing a beer while Samantha gestured and chattered away. They were too far away for Hannah to hear any of the conversation, but from what she could observe, Luke was in his own world. Did he blame himself for Adele's death? Or did he follow her to the beach to straighten her out and end up killing her in a fit of rage?

"When did Adele leave?"

Karla scrunched up her mouth. "It had to be after midnight. I'm pretty sure she finally left with that old guy."

That made sense to Hannah since Luke gave her a ride to the Pub and Pool Hall.

"Rory and I left about a half hour later."

"Did you stay at his apartment?"

"Now I wish I had, but he was in such a bad mood I had him drop me at my house."

"So Rory didn't have an alibi, or at least, *you* aren't his alibi."

Karla nodded. "Now I wish I didn't tell this to the police, but Rory told me he was planning to take a walk on the beach after he dropped me off. You know, to cool off."

Hannah forced herself to keep her face neutral but everything she heard about Rory sounded like the hole he was in just kept getting deeper.

Hannah patted Karla's hand. "Don't worry, I'll help Rory."

Hannah felt a heavy hand on her shoulder. "We need to talk." Her father's voice sent shivers up her spine as she slowly turned to face him.

This was her chance to ask him more about Adele but she wasn't sure she was ready to face his wrath.

Hannah followed her father back to the table in the corner where he had been sitting.

"Good luck," Samantha whispered as she passed Hannah and headed toward the pool table.

The chair was still warm when Hannah took the spot where Samantha had been sitting. She smiled at her father and pointed toward his glass of whiskey. "Drowning your sorrows?"

"Something like that."

Hannah watched his face but he wasn't giving anything away in his expression. Cold, gray eyes stared at her. His legs were crossed under the table. His left hand wrapped tightly around his glass was the only indication of any tension.

"Mom wants to leave."

"Of course she does. She always wants to run away from problems." He nursed his drink. "I'm not leaving until I finish my plan."

Hannah leaned across the table right in her father's face. "To take my land?"

He moved away from her. "To buy it." A grin crept into the edges of his mouth. "I heard your promise to help that pathetic sculptor friend of yours. You need money and I can help with that."

Hannah's stomach twisted. The beer was about to come out the way it had gone in, but she sucked in a deep breath and willed her body to cooperate. This must be his plan to force her to sell. "No thanks. I'd rather go to the bank."

Luke laughed and leaned close to Hannah. "The president of your bank is a good friend of mine and I've already had a chat with him about how overleveraged you are with your property. He loves my hotel idea."

The hairs on Hannah's neck rose. How did he know about her finances? It wasn't as if she was about to be foreclosed on, but she had borrowed to get her new cottage built and, at the moment, she was short for her next mortgage payment. She could play his game, though.

"You gave Adele a ride home from here the night, or rather, the morning before she was killed." Not a question, a statement that was bound to surprise him. "What's your alibi?"

"Your mother, of course."

Hannah shook her head. "I don't think so. She told me she never heard you come in. Maybe you didn't. A walk on the beach with Adele; argue with her about her drunken, unruly behavior; a handy shovel; smack her over the head in a fit of rage and use all your influence to blame an innocent person."

For a second, a shadow passed over Luke's face before he smirked. "You won't be able to sell that theory to anyone."

Hannah sat back and crossed her arms, her eyes glued to Luke's. "No? Someone saw you returning to your cottage."

He stared.

"I did. You were returning to the cottage early Saturday morning. I never saw you move so fast. Ever."

Luke stood up so fast his chair crashed backwards into the wall.

He stabbed his finger in Hannah's face.

She jerked her head away from him.

"Stop this foolishness now, Hannah. You never know what's good for you, and let me tell you for the last time, you will never win this battle."

For the first time in her life, Hannah stared back at her father knowing that somehow she *would* win this battle.

If she didn't, her whole life would be turned upside-down.

CHAPTER 13

Taste of Hooks Harbor should have been enough to get Hannah's salivary glands working in overdrive on Sunday, but after her conversation with her father the night before, preparing food was about the last thing she was looking forward to.

Unfortunately, The Fishy Dish had a tent at the event and Meg certainly didn't plan to run it herself.

By the time Hannah entered The Fishy Dish kitchen, Meg had bowls filled with various ingredients and boxes ready to be packed for transporting to the town green. She threw an apron to Hannah. "It's about time you dragged yourself out of bed. It wasn't *that* late last night, was it?"

Hannah tied the apron—lobster red with blue waves—around her neck and waist. "It wasn't too late but I couldn't get to sleep. I kept thinking about the fact that I saw my father drive into the parking lot here early Saturday morning and hurry to his cottage. I'm positive something happened and I'd put money on that whatever he was up to, it was connected to Adele."

Meg leaned against the counter. "Interesting. Moe told me he saw Luke near the marina. What doesn't make sense is that he said he saw you, too. Were you walking on the beach?"

"No. I walked to the beach right out here, but I never saw Moe." Hannah packed napkins and paper plates for the lobster rolls into a box. She straightened. "The bigger question is, what was Moe doing on the beach?"

"Watching the sunrise, or at least that's the line he gave me."

"Yeah, he told me that, too. Apparently, lots of people were on the beach early Saturday morning and one of them has to be the murderer." Hannah pulled lobster meat from the refrigerator.

"But Rory is the one who's locked up."

"And he needs a good lawyer."

"Does he have money for that?" Meg asked.

Hannah shook her head. "I've painted myself into a corner since I told Karla I would help."

Meg's eyes widened. "With what? You borrowed money to get your new cottage built."

"I know. I haven't figured it out yet. My hope is to get him out of jail before I have to cross that bridge."

Nellie, hanging out in front of the snack bar, woofed her friendly greeting, not her I-don't-know-who-you-are bark.

Cal strolled in with a tray filled with four coffees. "Anyone need a dose of caffeine?"

"You're a lifesaver. I haven't gotten any going here yet and, yes, caffeine is desperately needed." Meg helped herself to one of the coffees.

Hannah helped herself to another, Cal to a third. Hannah hoped Samantha would show up soon or the fourth cup would be cold. "Thanks. This isn't as strong as Jack's, but it's better than nothing."

"Girls night out last night?" Cal tilted his head as he looked at Hannah. She couldn't miss the sad expression in his eyes.

"Meg, Samantha, and I went to the Pub and Pool Hall." Hannah felt a tiny twinge of guilt that she hadn't told Cal her plans but she knew he would have insisted on coming, too.

"Interesting choice. Did you play any pool?"

"I did, and I got my head handed to me on a platter," Meg said. "That sculptor from Florida is pretty slick but I made sure to tell him that I *let* him win. You know, I didn't want his fragile ego to explode when an older woman beat him."

Cal chuckled. "And did he buy it?"

"No, but it gave Hannah time to chat with Karla and her dad without any interruptions."

"Karla told me that Rory was planning to take a walk on the beach after he dropped her off after they left the Pub and Pool Hall. He did everything wrong—

argued with Adele after he lost, left his shovel where someone could find it, and put himself right at the scene of the crime." She shook her head. "And I promised to help him pay for a lawyer." She slapped her forehead, letting him know without saying anything that she knew that was a mistake. Not only did she not have the money, but she barely knew the guy. She just knew her dad couldn't be right.

"What if Rory is guilty, Hannah? Have you considered that possibility?" Cal asked.

Hannah's head dropped. "Yes, of course that's a possibility. But from what I've heard about Rory, what Karla told me, in my heart I don't think he's capable of murder. Could I be wrong? I hope not." What she left unsaid was that if she *was* wrong about Rory, she might end up losing her property to her father to help Rory pay for a lawyer. She would do it because she promised and she would honor that promise.

Samantha arrived in a hot pink t-shirt and white capris. "Your father sure was a bore last night. Is he always like that?" she asked Hannah. "I don't think he heard any of my stories.

"No, usually he's the life of a party but he had his mind on something else," Hannah said. How to steal her property, most likely.

Samantha clapped her hands. She obviously didn't need the coffee Cal had brought for her but she pick up the cup anyway. "Okay then. Let's get this show on the road. What's ready to carry out to Cal's truck?"

"Someone woke up bright eyed and raring to go," Meg said. She pointed to a stack of boxes and a couple of coolers. "You can start with that stuff. Make sure the coolers are wedged in tight and don't go sliding around when Cal has to slam on his brakes to avoid a clueless tourist."

"Right. We need every hungry vacationer to devour all the lobster rolls you're making plus all the gallons of clam chowder, and it looks like you've got a ton of potatoes cut up for fries. I predict that to be the hot seller today." Hannah closed the box she'd packed and added it on top of the other boxes.

"Don't forget my coleslaw. I know it's only a side, but it always disappears." Samantha said.

Meg and Hannah finished packing while Samantha and Cal lugged all the boxes, coolers, tables, and a portable stove to his truck.

When it was just the two of them in the kitchen, Meg asked, "Do you have much to go on about this murder?"

Hannah sighed. "My father, Rory, Moe, and Karla on the beach early Saturday morning, Rory's shovel that anyone could have grabbed, and a mermaid necklace that belonged to the victim but showed up around Karla's neck."

Meg whipped her head around. "How did Karla get Adele's necklace? That sounds like an important clue."

"I know. There's three possibilities. Moe told Pam that Adele gave it back to him when they split up and he gave it to Karla. Or either Moe or Karla took it from Adele after she was dead."

"If Adele gave it back to Moe, would he actually re-gift it to another woman?" Meg's voice dripped with disgust.

"He does come across as the kind of guy who might do something like that, but I don't think Adele would ever return a gift. When she showed up here at The Fishy Dish before the competition, she rubbed that mermaid like it was some kind of lucky charm. I know her. She wasn't one to give anything back."

"So you're focused on Moe as the killer?"

Hannah sipped her now lukewarm coffee. "What I think is that Moe likes to act like this cool, together dude but he doesn't like to lose. He reminds me of my father. And men like that go for revenge. He lost the sand sculpting competition to a woman who recently dumped him or, at the very least, was toying with his emotions. Maybe part of her game was to beat him, show him she was better than he was at something they both loved."

"And he could have taken Rory's shovel when the competition was over, stuck it near his stuff, and bided his time," Meg added.

"It wouldn't be a stretch for Moe to assume that Adele would take one last walk by her mermaid sculpture before the tide washed it away forever. Both Moe and my father must have known that vanity streak in her."

"Wow, Hannah, it all makes sense. No wonder you haven't been able to sleep. You know too much about the victim."

"Right, but how do I prove it? All the evidence is pointing to Rory. What I said is only theory. Except the necklace. There has to be more about that necklace. Maybe a photo or something showing Adele still wearing it well after when Moe said he saw her."

"That's it! Someone must have taken photos of the winning sculpture. I'll check with Michael to find out if he took any pictures when everyone was at the Pub and Pool Hall. He likes to chronical events that way."

"What are you two doing in here?" Samantha asked. "You haven't gotten any more boxes ready to go."

"Right." Meg scraped the last of the hand-cut potatoes into a big plastic container. "We got sidetracked trying to figure out what happened to the silver mermaid."

Samantha scrunched her eyebrows.

"Adele's necklace," Hannah explained. "It could be the missing puzzle piece."

As they loaded the last of the supplies into Cal's truck for transporting to the Taste of Hooks Harbor event, Hannah's parents walked to their rental car.

Joanna smiled at Hannah. "We'll see you in town? My mouth is watering thinking about a tasty lobster roll."

"Thanks, Mom. Is your headache gone?"

"Yes. I took another long walk on the beach early this morning and I think the fresh ocean air blew the last remnants of that nasty migraine out to sea."

Luke sat in the driver's seat without even looking at his daughter. "Come on Joanna. I need my coffee."

Joanna rolled her eyes so only Hannah could see. "See you later, honey."

Hannah watched the car pull out of the parking lot and she got an idea. "You guys get started with the set up without me. I just remembered something important I need to do."

Meg leaned close. "It doesn't have anything to do with the *Something's Fishy* cottage, does it?"

"It might. I'll let you know if I find what I think I will."

Hannah and Nellie made a beeline to *Something's Fishy* as soon as the dust from Cal's truck settled. She used her master key to enter. Her nerves jangled with anticipation and a dash of fear.

Joanna's iPad was tucked in the top drawer of the dresser, just as Hannah suspected. She opened it and keyed in one two one two, her mother's birthday and what she always used for an easy-to-remember password. Success! She clicked on the photos icon and found exactly what she expected. All the photos that Joanna and Luke took on their phones ended up on Joanna's iPad.

Photos of Adele loaded on the screen. Adele while she did her sculpting. Adele while she accepted the winner's award. Adele at the Pub and Pool Hall. Adele sitting in Luke's rental car.

In every photo, the mermaid necklace was draped around Adele's neck. She couldn't have *given* it back to Moe, at least not until sometime between midnight on Friday and when she was killed in the early morning hours of Saturday.

How did Karla end up with it, then?

CHAPTER 14

By the time Hannah arrived at the town green for the Taste of Hooks Harbor event, she could see that The Fishy Dish tent was all set up. Meg bustled around getting ready for the opening at eleven. Aromas wafted through the air, mixing together to get anyone's appetite kicked into high gear. Clam chowder, spicy barbeque, freshly baked bread, and a big variety of desserts to satisfy any sweet tooth drifted from all the tents as Hannah walked by. Laughter, kids screeching happily, and music filtered through the background. And a brilliant blue sky with a few puffy white clouds filled the backdrop for the illusion, at least, that everything was right with the world.

"Got a minute?" Pam, in her police uniform, tapped Hannah on her shoulder.

Hannah stopped and they moved away from the crowd.

"We still have Rory. I heard you're helping him pay for a lawyer?"

"If I have to I will but I'm hoping it doesn't come to that."

Pam raised her eyebrows and peered over the top of her glasses at Hannah. "Do you know something I don't know?"

"Something doesn't add up about that mermaid necklace that belonged to Adele but ended up around Karla's neck. Moe told you Adele gave it back to him, but when? I saw photos of Adele wearing the necklace until past midnight Friday night."

"I agree with you that something smells rotten with that picture. I'll need to see those photos. We're keeping our eyes on Moe ever since he almost skipped town."

"But the murder weapon belonged to Rory so he's your number one suspect," Hannah said matter-of-factly.

"Exactly. For now."

"Anyone could have taken that shovel at some point, Pam. What about Moe or Karla? Or even my father?"

"I'm still checking details of their statements but I had to take a break for an early lunch. Does Meg have lobster rolls on the menu at your tent?"

"She certainly does. Come on and I'll personally make you the biggest, most tender, and tastiest lobster roll you've ever had." Hannah smiled. "With one condition."

Pam stopped walking. "Um, I'm not sure I can agree to any conditions."

"Bring one for Rory?"

Pam hesitated before answering. "Okay. Put two in a bag and I'll make sure he gets one."

"Thanks." Hannah put her hand on Pam's arm. "Rory is innocent. Someone is setting him up."

"I hope you're right. He's a good kid with a lot of talent, but be careful what you wish for, Hannah. *Someone* is the murderer and you may not like the alternative if Rory is cleared."

Hannah hadn't considered that possibility. What if her father was the murderer? Or Karla? She had been assuming it was Moe all along.

"Hurry up and get me the lobster rolls. I have to get back to work." Pam moved at a fast clip toward The Fishy Dish tent and Hannah had to jog to catch up.

While Pam chatted with Jack, who had just arrived at the tent, Hannah assembled two giant lobster rolls, wrapped them up tightly, and tucked them inside a paper bag for Pam. "Do you want fries with that, too?"

Pam gave Hannah a what-kind-of-question look is that.

Hannah dumped an extra-large serving of fries into a separate bag, dumped on salt, and threw in several little packs of ketchup. "Share these."

Pam saluted and took the two bags.

"You two are getting along now?" Jack asked, his face silently telling her, I can't believe what I just saw.

"We've moved to a new level. Ever since, you know." She mouthed *Caroline* as her eyes darted around the crowd to be sure no one was reading her lips. Would she ever get used to keeping this secret?

"I get it. We're all on the same team now."

Olivia darted between Hannah and Jack and wrapped her arms around Hannah's legs. "Mom is so mean," she sobbed.

Ruby looked at Hannah and rolled her eyes at the comment.

Hannah crouched down to her niece's eye level. "That's part of a mom's job description, Olivia. If moms aren't a tiny bit mean every once in a while, they don't get a good grade on their Mom Report Card."

Olivia's face crunched into a pile of wrinkles. "It's not fair. Grandpa wants to take me to the aquarium in Boston. I want to see all the fishies." Her voice wailed out the last word pitifully.

"Hey, I've got an idea. How about Cal and I take you instead? We can see the big tank with the sharks, fishies, and turtles. Cal has never been so I'll treat you both."

Olivia's eyes lit up like two little lightning bugs. "Really? Can we bring Theodore, too? He told me he wants to see the sharks."

"Sure." Hannah ruffled Olivia's hair. "But you have to promise not to drop that bear into the tank."

Olivia, her face deadly serious, nodded. "I'll hold on tight, tight, tight. Just like this." She squeezed her teddy bear with a six-year-old death grip.

Hannah laughed. "As soon as I get all moved into my new cottage, we'll take a day off. Do you think it would be okay for your mom to come, too?"

Olivia's head bobbed up and down. "Mom would *love* it. There's Cal. I'll tell him." Olivia darted away.

"Can you really get away?" Ruby asked Hannah. "Olivia won't forget this promise. You'll break her heart if you don't keep it."

"I think I've earned a day off. Maybe next week? Can Olivia play hooky from school for one day?"

"As long as you don't make a habit of it. How are you going to tell Dad? He won't be thrilled that you stole his idea and upstaged him."

Hannah shrugged. "Too bad for him. He has to learn to play by our rules."

"I hope you know what you're doing. Dad doesn't forgive easily when he's crossed."

"I know, but it's time we stand up to him. Don't you think? I'm tired of having him push me around." Hannah pulled her long braid over her shoulder and rubbed the end between her thumb and finger. "Do you think maybe Adele crossed him and he went for revenge?"

"What are you two chatting about over here?" Joanna pushed between Hannah and Ruby, draping an arm over each of her daughters' shoulders.

Hannah's heart skipped a beat. What did Joanna hear? "Are you ready for that lobster roll?" she asked, hoping her mom would drop her curiosity about her and Ruby's conversation wondering about the possibility of Luke killing Adele. Joanna would most certainly be appalled over that speculation.

"Yes. I'm ravenous. Can you make two? Your father doesn't want to ask, but I know it's one of his favorites."

"Where is he?"

Joanna flicked her wrist. "He had some business at the bank. I told him I'd get us lunch before we take a drive up the coast. It's a beautiful day for a drive, don't you think?"

Hearing that Luke went to the bank didn't sit well with Hannah and the comments he made to her last night. Could he sway his friend there to say no to loaning her any more money? That thought would have to wait.

Hannah hadn't seen her mother so cheerful since she'd arrived. "You must be feeling much better, Mom."

"I am." Joanna looked into Hannah's eyes. "It's sad about Adele but maybe you and your father can get along now?"

"Are you serious? Adele has never been a favorite of mine, but there's nothing that makes it okay for her to be murdered." Hannah pulled her mother to the side of the tent. "Dad was out early Saturday morning. Is there any chance he had anything to do with Adele's death?"

Joanna's mouth dropped open. "You can't be serious. Your father and Adele were," she paused to find the right word. "They were very close. Don't the police have that local boy in custody?"

"Yes, but I don't think he killed Adele. Someone set him up and I'm going to get to the bottom of it."

"Oh, Hannah, honey. Can't you leave it to the police? What if you put yourself into danger by digging into this mess?"

"What if I *don't* dig into this mess and the wrong person is charged with a crime he didn't commit? I could *never* forgive myself if I didn't do everything possible." Hannah couldn't believe how cavalier her mother had become about Adele. Although, it was consistent with her aversion to drama. She only wanted everyone and everything in her small world to be in harmony. Too bad life didn't work that way.

"Listen, Mom, I have a favor to ask."

"Of course, I'll do anything I can to help."

"Did you or Dad take photos of Adele during the sand sculpting competition and when you took her out to dinner?" Hannah knew the answer to the question but she wanted those photos without resorting to stealing them from her mother's iPad.

"That's a silly question. You know we chronicle everything. Your father and I both have lots of photos of Adele on our iPads. Why?" Joanna's dark brown eyes searched Hannah's face.

Hannah shrugged. "No reason except that I'd like to see them."

"Okay. I'll leave my iPad in your office before we leave for our drive. Can you get the lobster rolls made before your father wonders if I disappeared off the face of the earth?"

Hannah scooped the lobster salad from the bowl and piled it into two toasted rolls. The small hurdle of getting her mother's photos of Adele went much more smoothly than she imagined. "Here you go. Enjoy," she said as she handed a bag with two lobster rolls to her mother.

"There's something I'd like to ask you to do for me." Joanna waited.

Hannah didn't like the harder tone in her mother's voice.

"Convince Ruby to let us take Olivia to Boston. She seemed so excited about going to the aquarium and your father thinks it would be a wonderful way for us to bond with her."

"I can't do that, Mom. Olivia barely knows you two and it's a long trip for her. Besides, it's not my place to tell Ruby how to parent her daughter."

Joanna's face remained emotionless. "I'm sorry you feel that way." She took the offered bag. "I've changed my mind about my iPad. I'll need to take it with us today so I can take photos." Joanna turned and left without letting Hannah have another word in the discussion.

She told herself she should have known it was too good to be true when her mother was so willing to share her iPad. Her parents always wanted something in return for a favor. Her father *and* her mother. The difference was that her father demanded and threatened. Her mother only took something away to make a point.

Hannah shoved the lobster salad bowl back into the cooler and let the lid slam closed. Those photos were an important clue. She'd get another look at them one way or another.

CHAPTER 15

"What was that all about?" Jack leaned into the side of the work area toward Hannah.

"Typical family power play. My mom's getting into the act now, pressuring us to let Olivia go to Boston with them for the day."

Jack's eyes widened. "Ruby isn't letting her go, is she?"

"Of course not. Even without Great Aunt Caroline's warning ringing in my ear, I wouldn't let Ruby trust them with Olivia. They didn't do the greatest job with us, and the least we can do is protect her from being a victim to those mistakes a second time."

"I'm keeping my eyes on her, too. Just in case. It's so busy here, she could disappear in the blink of an eye." He began to walk away.

"Jack?"

He stopped and turned toward Hannah.

"How long will Ruby and I have to live like this? You know, looking over our shoulders and worrying about Olivia?"

"I don't have the answer to that question. But don't forget how well Nellie guards her, too. When Caroline sent Nellie to watch out for you, she didn't know she'd get twice the bang from her gift. Your folks won't stay in Hooks Harbor forever. They love to travel too much."

"Thankfully," Hannah said before a customer got her attention with an order for a bowl of clam chowder.

The rush was on for chowder and lobster rolls with sides of creamy coleslaw and salty French fries. In the small tent area, it was a challenge to keep up. But somehow, Meg, Hannah, and Samantha danced around each other without stepping on each other's toes. Too many times.

"That's why I told you to leave your flip flops home," Meg reminded Hannah after the heel of her foot squished Hannah's little toe. "Maybe next time you'll listen to me."

"Hey, I've been over here waiting forever. How about some fries and a bowl of that fish soup you make."

Moe Meyer's voice grated in Hannah's ears. At least she didn't smell the annoying cigarette odor. But when she turned in his direction, he grinned and lit a cigarette. He used it to salute toward Hannah.

"Did you mean my clam chowder?" Hannah asked without hiding the annoyance in her voice.

"Yeah, whatever it is. Ya got a minute to spare?"

"Kinda busy." Hannah filled a cup with steaming chowder, grabbed a package of oyster crackers, and handed both to Moe. "Spoons are at the front of the tent."

"Too busy to hear some interesting information? About Adele?" Moe's mouth stretched into a smile but his eyes projected a dark, piercing glare. With a nod of his head, he added, "I'll be over on that bench enjoying this if you decide you have time to hear what I've got to share."

Hannah wiped sweat off her brow and watched Moe saunter to the edge of the green. He made himself comfortable on a bench. He crossed his legs and opened the chowder container.

Hannah untied her apron. "Meg, I have to leave for a few minutes to find out what information Moe Meyers is ready to share."

"Don't get taken in by what he says. He probably wants to save his own skin."

"I'll listen." Hannah carried a big cone of hot French fries with her. Eating and sharing might help build a tiny bit of trust.

Moe's face broke into a wide grin when Hannah stood in front of him. His shaggy, sun-bleached hair and casual attitude projected a model's image. "I can tell you're the kind of guy who likes to be in control." She tilted her head. "Is that why Adele dumped you? She never let *anyone* have any control over her."

The words wiped the grin right off his face. Moe uncrossed his legs and leaned toward Hannah. "It took me too long to understand that Adele was *only* about Adele. There was no room for anyone else."

"I couldn't agree with you more. We went to high school together, you know." Hannah sat next to Moe and offered him some fries. She was beginning to feel a tiny bit of comradery with this person who'd also landed on the wrong side of Adele Bailey.

"Yeah, she told me she was looking forward to seeing you again."

Hannah frowned. "Really? She hated me."

Moe helped himself to several fries. "Really? She hoped you had gained about fifty pounds and turned into an ugly spinster. When I first saw you, I was kind of shocked, to be perfectly honest. The way Adele described you, the last thing I expected to see was a beautiful, athletic, sun-tanned woman. And then you yelled at me about my cigarette butt and I knew we'd be friends at some point."

Hannah stared at Moe and then burst out laughing. "Well, I'm glad I disappointed her. But, friends with you? Probably not." She dug into her fries with gusto. Even though Adele had commented on the fact that she gained a few pounds, as far as Hannah was concerned, those pounds were all muscle from the hard work of running her business.

After a not-too-uncomfortable stretch of silence, while Moe crumbled the oyster crackers into the chowder and Hannah polished off the bulk of the fries, she asked, "Why did you follow her on the beach early Saturday morning? To try to finally get in the last word or something?"

Moe poured the last bit of chowder into his mouth, sighed and leaned back. "Pretty good, maybe even the best I've ever had."

"Thanks. We win every competition we enter." She bit her tongue to be patient while Moe decided how to answer her question.

"Yes, I did follow Adele. Or, rather, I suspected she might be back at her mermaid sand sculpture to admire her work if it was still together, so that's where I went. She would want to savor every last minute with her award-winning work before it disappeared under the tide." He shrugged. "I couldn't sleep, anyway, and it was a nice night for a moonlit walk on the beach."

"You found her where you expected?"

"I did. She was angry and attacked me, saying men were all evil and she couldn't trust any of them." He turned sideways and looked at Hannah. "It was weird to say the least. I had never seen her like that."

"Too much to drink?"

"Possibly. I got her somewhat calmed down and that was when she threw the mermaid necklace in the sand at my feet. She said she was leaving as soon as the sun came up. No hug, no good bye, no *have a nice life*. She didn't even say it was fun while it lasted."

Hannah realized she was holding her breath. Was Moe going to admit to killing Adele?

"I picked up the necklace and walked away."

"So Adele was still alive at, what time was that?"

"Around four a.m. maybe. I didn't pay attention. It was before the sun came up. And, yes, Adele was still angry and very much alive."

"Where did you go?"

"I walked toward the marina and that's when I saw you, or, at least I thought it was you. There was someone in the distance, about your size, long hair."

"She was walking in Adele's direction?"

"Uh-huh. I remember thinking, someone else for her to rip apart. It actually made me feel good that I wasn't the only one to be on the receiving end of her wrath."

Hannah stood. "Why are you telling me all this?"

"When I thought Rory was the murderer, I didn't care, but now I'm worried. About Karla. She was so eager to get out of town, and don't get me wrong, I'd love for her to come with me, but not if it means she's running away from something that might haunt us down the road."

"Murder? You think that woman you saw walking toward Adele was Karla? And she's the killer?" Hannah asked. She sagged back down onto the bench.

"I just don't know, but you're the one digging under every nook and cranny so I figured you should have all the information I have."

Hannah was stunned. Karla on the beach twice? Once to kill Adele. She would know exactly where Rory's shovel was kept. Then an early morning run to "find" Adele's body? It would be clever to throw off the police. Did she intend to incriminate Rory and get out of town any way possible before any clues pointed in her direction?

Or was Moe the clever one to try to throw the police and Hannah off *his* trail? He couldn't prove the story he just told her about arguing with Adele and walking away while Adele was still alive. His story could be truth or fiction. Unless she could find a witness, she might never know. She would have to talk to Karla and find out where she went and what she saw. Or if she even admitted to being near the marina at four a.m. Saturday morning.

CHAPTER 16

Meg drained the last of the chowder into a serving bowl. For herself. She crumbled three packs of oyster crackers over the top. "Don't look at me like that. After this busy day, I deserve the last bowl with all the big pieces of clams that sank to the bottom," she said to Hannah, trying not to sound guilty for being selfish.

"I'm famished, but don't worry about me," Hannah replied, trying to keep a straight face.

"I worked harder than anyone around here. I earned it." But Meg poured half of the chowder into another bowl and handed it to Hannah. "Here. If you don't take it, I won't be able to enjoy this pitiful amount that's left."

Hannah happily accepted the container and hungrily devoured the treat.

Between spoonfuls, Meg said, "We sold a *lot* of clam chowder today, a ton of my super-duper salty hand-cut fries, and all the brochures about your business are gone. Remind me whose great idea it was to participate in the Taste of Hooks Harbor event this year?"

"As a matter of fact, I recall Jack telling me about it first."

"Jack? Are you kidding? *I* told Jack how we should have a tent and spread the word about The Fishy Dish.

Lots of people said they'd stop by. I suspect they might be hoping to sit under one of your umbrellas with an ice cream while a body floats up on the beach. It's all everyone could talk about today—who murdered that beautiful sculptress?"

"They want more bodies to show up? What's wrong with everyone?" Hannah shuddered at the thought. If there was another body it very well could be hers with the reputation she had for snooping for clues.

"Who knows? Everyone is shocked to the core, but for some reason they want to be in the middle of the excitement." Meg packed her dirty pots and utensils into a box, folded the red-and-white checkered tablecloths over the top, and started to break down the folding tables. "Where's Cal? He can start lugging this stuff to his truck."

Hannah stretched on her tippy toes and spotted him on the far side of the green, walking with Samantha. She waved her arm to get his attention. "He's on his way." She helped Meg dismantle the rest of the tables and leaned them against the tent pole.

Cal picked up some trash next to the tent. "Ruby and Olivia went home. Jack is heading to the office in case anyone at the cottages needs anything. What's ready to go to my truck?"

Meg handed Samantha a box and led the way to Cal's truck, leaving Hannah and Cal to dismantle the tent.

"Did you hear about Rory?" Cal asked Hannah.

She froze. "No. What happened? Did he get charged with murder?"

"No. Jack told me he's free to go home but not leave town. There were too many fingerprints on his shovel and a witness turned up to verify he wasn't on the beach at the time of Adele's murder."

"What witness?"

"A friend of Rory's."

Hannah frowned. "Why did it take so long?"

Cal shrugged. "I saw you talking to Moe for quite a while."

"He gave me the impression he thinks Karla might be the murderer. He said he saw her near the marina walking toward where he had just had a chat with Adele around four a.m. Saturday morning. At least he *thinks* it was Karla. At first he thought it was me so I don't think his eye-witness testimony is worth much."

"People are hard to figure out. So what is the truth?"

"And who else left fingerprints on that shovel?" Hannah shook her head. Her long braid swished back and forth across her shoulder blades. "I need to find out if anyone saw Moe on the beach. So far, he seems to be the only one seeing other people."

"Geez, you two," Meg said when she returned for the third time from lugging boxes to Cal's truck. "Samantha and I are working our butts off and you haven't even gotten the tent down."

Hannah and Cal made quick work taking the tent apart while Meg took the last box to the truck. The green had only a few tourists meandering through. All the vendors were long-gone by the time Cal carried the folded tent and poles to his truck.

"See you at your new cottage? We could put our feet up, enjoy the view, and have a cold drink," Cal asked.

"Ahhh. That sounds like Heaven. See you there," Hannah replied. Her shoulders sagged. Her pace was slow and she hoped nothing interfered with the rest of her day.

Of course that was not how things worked. Wanting something and getting something are not the same thing.

As Hannah drove toward her paradise, Karla trudged along the side of the road. Part of Hannah's brain screamed, just keep driving, your boyfriend is waiting with a delicious cold drink, but as so often happened, the other half of her brain didn't listen.

She pulled her Volvo over, rolled down the window, and said, "Hop in. I'll give you a ride." Hannah had no idea where Karla was headed. But this unexpected opportunity to ask her some questions about Adele was too important to let pass by.

Karla hesitated. She looked up and down the road as if she was calculating whether a better ride might come along. No cars even slowed down. Karla opened the door and slid into the passenger seat, her mind made up and giving the impression that this was an important decision.

"Where are you going?" Hannah asked as she started driving.

Karla shrugged. "Just trying to get away from everything." She turned sideways and stared at Hannah. "You must know what it's like."

"What, *what's* like?" Something was about to spill out of Karla but Hannah couldn't even begin to know what direction it was heading.

"To have everyone try to tell you what they think is best for you." She mimicked someone in a bossy tone. "Stay here in Hooks Harbor. Get a job. Settle down. Raise a family. You'll never survive on your own in a city. You know, that kind of advice. My parents tell me what to do instead of letting me follow my dreams. Even if it doesn't work out. Can't they let me figure that out on my own?"

Hannah was stunned. What Karla said was true, but how did she know Hannah's parents, especially her father, told her those exact pieces of so-called advice? "Why would you think I could relate to that?"

Karla laughed. "Your father gave me a ride and all he could talk about was how you've ruined your life by living here and running your business. Maybe all parents tell their kids the same thing but it sounded like the same broken record that I heard over and over from my own father, the same exasperation I heard when he got on a roll about what I *should* do with my life. And, especially, what I *shouldn't* do, which is exactly what I *want* to do."

"My father gave you a ride? That doesn't sound like him at all."

"It was kind of weird. I was out walking early on Saturday morning, looking for Rory, and your father drove by. I suppose he thought it wasn't safe for a young woman to be out alone. Anyway, I was about to give up looking, so I let him give me a ride to Rory's apartment. That seemed like the best place to wait for him. I had to listen to his complaining about you as payment for the ride."

"Did he say what *he* was doing out driving around so early?"

"I didn't ask. I didn't really care at that point. I wanted to find out if Rory still planned to leave town so I could figure out my own plans. Everything got turned upside down when *Adele*," she spit out Adele's name like it was a mouthful of boiling hot chowder, "won the competition. And the money. We were counting on using the prize money to get started in Boston." She flung her hands to the sides. "I never told Rory I had some money saved up. I wanted to hear his plan first."

"So you're heading to Boston? By yourself?" Hannah tried not to sound judgmental like Karla's father. It wasn't easy.

"Not yet. Actually, I was planning to stop by your place before I left."

"Oh?" That comment caught Hannah by surprise. "I guess my driving by when I did was a bit of fate."

"You believe in that stuff?" Karla snickered. "I saw you were packing your stuff up on the green and figured you'd be heading in this direction. So, not exactly fate. More like logical reasoning. I decided I'd find a ride with you or with whoever stopped first and you won."

Hannah pulled into The Fishy Dish parking lot. She held Karla's arm. "Before we leave the car and get distracted by all the other people here, tell me what you wanted to talk to me about."

"You didn't figure it out already? What was your father doing driving around early Saturday morning? At the time I couldn't have cared less, but that was *before* I knew about Adele. He gave Adele a ride to the Pub and Pool Hall, they had a loud argument there, but she left with him anyway. What happened after they left?"

What indeed, Hannah wondered. Too many suspects were seen near the beach early Saturday morning. Too many that could have a motive to murder Adele. And all of them pointing their finger toward someone else.

Including Karla.

Dumb luck in getting picked up by her father while she was looking for Rory?

Or premeditated murder.

Karla slid out of Hannah's car. "Thanks for the ride." She bent down to tie the laces on her running shoes. "It will only take me about twenty minutes to run back to the marina from here. Rory should be waiting at his apartment."

"Wait a minute." Hannah looked at Karla over the top of her car. "What about Moe? Weren't you planning to go to Florida with him? How's Rory going to feel about that decision on your part?"

Karla shrugged. "What he doesn't know won't hurt him." Her eyes narrowed as she met Hannah's gaze. "And he won't know unless you tell him. Stay out of my life." With that veiled threat, she took several long strides toward the beach and broke into a loping run with her ponytail swinging like a pendulum across her back. It reminded Hannah of a ticking clock, and the clock was ticking down.

Hannah watched until she was out of sight.

"I worried you got lost." Cal's voice interrupted Hannah's thoughts. His arm rested on her shoulder.

"No, just distracted. I gave Karla a ride and our conversation left a bad taste in my mouth."

"Karla? She comes across as young and a bit innocent, but not someone I would expect to be controversial."

"I know. Maybe she's only being opportunistic. Now that Rory's out of jail, Moe's off her radar and she's running back to Rory. I don't like how she seems to be using him as her get-out-of-town card."

"Well, you have something else to distract you."

Hannah turned her head to look up into Cal's face.

"Your parents are waiting to take you, Ruby, and Olivia out for dinner. They aren't taking no for an answer according to Ruby."

Hannah groaned. "I knew I wouldn't be able to put them off forever. Don't you want to come, too?"

"Sorry. I'm not invited. Ruby already tried to include me but your father said it's a *family* thing."

"Typical. Unless, of course, Adele was still alive. He always considered *her* part of our family."

"Why?" Cal asked.

"I don't know. My parents were close to her parents, and since she didn't have siblings, she just always seemed to be included in our adventures. It was fine at first, but once her competitive streak blossomed, I dreaded every second I had to be near her. My father admired that in her, of course, and pushed me and Ruby to be more like Adele. Ugh. What it accomplished was to make me less competitive which made my once-decent relationship with my father spiral downhill. I put more value on a close relationship with a deeper meaning instead of one that was based on winning and beating another person at all costs."

Cal pulled Hannah close. "That's a healthier and longer-lasting outlook." His eyes twinkled. "I'll have to thank your father for teaching you that lesson."

Hannah laughed. "Only if you want to be on his bad side."

They walked arm-in-arm toward the picnic tables. "I think you should come with us. I don't care what my father said. As far as I'm concerned, you're family to me, Ruby, and Olivia."

Cal's eyebrows raised.

"My father can just deal with it. The new me took a page out of Great Aunt Caroline's life and I'm not letting him push me around, remember?"

"I *like* this new you. I've noticed that you've acquired more of Caroline's strengths every day. And that's a huge compliment."

CHAPTER 17

Hannah squeezed Cal's hand, letting his confidence flow into her hand and ultimately to her core as they approached her parents, waiting in front of The Fishy Dish.

"There you are." Joanna rose and hugged Hannah. "I'm sure you're tired after your busy day so Dad and I want to take you girls," she obviously excluded Cal, "to dinner tonight."

"Great." Hannah forced her mouth into a smile. "Cal's coming with us and I'd like to go to the Pub and Pool Hall. It's about time I teach Olivia how to play a little pool."

Ruby's eyes widened but she said nothing. Apparently, she planned to let Hannah handle the situation even though a pool hall wasn't the greatest environment for a six-year-old. They'd figure that out as the night wore on.

"Oh," Joanna said. "That doesn't sound like a very fancy establishment. Wouldn't you like to go somewhere...nicer?"

"The owner, Michael, is a good friend of mine and I like to support his business. Besides, Dad went there with Adele Friday night. If it's good enough for Dad, it's good enough for us, right Ruby?"

"Sure. They have pizza so Olivia will be happy."

Olivia jumped up and down with the excitement of doing anything out of the normal routine. "Theodore likes pizza, too."

"Oh dear, another person is coming? Who is Theodore?" Joanna wrung her hands, obviously in a dilemma with this growing crowd barging in and potentially ruining her family dinner plans.

Olivia held up her teddy bear. "Theodore isn't a people, Grandma. He's my teddy. He's thirty and he lived with Cal but now he lives with me and I take him everywhere."

"That's nice, honey." Joanna patted Olivia's head. "What do you think, Luke?" Joanna pulled Luke into the negotiations and waited for him to weigh in on the situation that was *not* going as she had hoped.

Hannah felt her father's eyes studying her face. She kept her expression neutral. He was the one who taught her how to hide her emotions, how to fool someone else during a game of cards, but he also had always been able to read her. She didn't know if that was still true.

Without taking his eyes off Hannah's face he answered, "Hannah and I haven't played pool in far too long. The Pub and Pool Hall sounds perfect. We might even be able to throw a little wager on the game. You know, to keep it interesting." A smile spread across his lips but his eyes remained cold and challenging. "What do you say, Hannah?"

She rubbed the gold band on her finger, channeling Great Aunt Caroline's strength, and stared right back at her father. She didn't know how, but it felt like strength seeped through the precious metal into her own body. Great Aunt Caroline's strength would get her through the night. "I'm glad you like my idea," she replied.

Luke blinked first.

Hannah smiled. She was strong and confident. "I'll meet you there after I take a quick shower and walk Nellie. Forty-five minutes?"

"Six-thirty, sharp," Luke answered. "I'll have the game set up and ready to go."

Hannah headed toward her cottage, followed by Ruby, Cal, and Olivia. Once they were all inside, with the door closed, Ruby finally said something. "What was that all about? Are you and Dad in some kind of power struggle?"

Hannah chuckled. "You could say that. I'm pretty sure he plans on trying to win this property from me in a game of pool."

"You can't risk that, Hannah," Ruby shouted.

"I can and I will. I have to end this problem, once and for all, or we'll always be looking over our shoulders. Dad always expected to inherit this property and he will undermine me in every way possible. Unless I beat him in this game. I *plan* to win." She walked into her bathroom and shut the door.

She sat on the edge of the tub with her head in her hands, wondering what she had just done. Sure, she sounded confident even to her own ears, but it wasn't how she felt inside. Was she about to make the biggest mistake of her life?

The hot water pounded on her head, shoulders, and back. She forced her mind to concentrate on the pulsing drops and nothing else. A calm wrapped around her like a warm embrace.

By the time she finished her shower, pulled on her favorite comfy jeans and t-shirt, Hannah was ready for her challenge.

Cal opened the cottage door and entered with Nellie when Hannah emerged from her shower. "I took her for a walk so you don't have to do that. Ruby and Olivia went home. We'll pick them up on our way by." He put his hands on Hannah's shoulders. "Are you okay? You've got an enormous challenge ahead if you're right about your father."

"I'm as ready as I'll ever be. See what I'm wearing?"

Cal looked at Hannah's shirt and chuckled. "*I know I play like a girl, try to keep up,*" Cal read. "I'm guessing you chose that t-shirt to get under your father's thin skin. I hope you know what you're doing."

"Me too." She smiled. "Let's go."

"Oh, I almost forgot to tell you. Jack and Meg will be there, too. For moral support. And Jack said he might bring someone else along. A surprise guest."

"The more the merrier," Hannah said enthusiastically. She was *so* ready for this showdown with her father. She couldn't help but wonder if Great Aunt Caroline was about to make some sort of appearance. But that would be much too risky.

Ruby and Olivia dashed outside as soon as Cal's truck pulled up in front of their house. They squeezed into the back seat.

Olivia chattered nonstop to Theodore, explaining what she could see outside the truck window and reminding him that pizza was the treat for dinner.

"Mom brought up the subject of a trip again," Ruby leaned over the front seat and whispered quietly into Hannah's ear. "Should we invite them with us when we go?"

"Maybe. Let's see how tonight goes."

Cal's hand found Hannah's and he squeezed her fingers. Butterflies fluttered in the pit of her stomach but she told herself nerves always made her play better. What the others didn't know was that Hannah was in money trouble with her business. Her plan was to use this opportunity to get out of debt, get out from under her father's agenda, and maybe even teach Olivia a bit about pool all at the same time.

Cal's truck lurched across a giant pot hole throwing everyone off the seats.

"I don't remember that one. Where do all these holes come from?" Cal asked without expecting an answer.

"Maybe it's where the mermaids come from," Olivia offered. "Did you see the mermaid on the beach?"

"That wasn't real, honey," Ruby said.

"Yes it was. Grandpa told me he saw her move."

"It' time for Grandpa to get glasses."

"He *talked* to her, too. He told me all about her and how she was moving away and never talking to him again."

Hannah turned her head and caught Ruby's gaze. They both raised their eyebrows. "Is that why he wants to go to the aquarium? To find his mermaid friend?" Olivia continued.

"I don't know but, remember? Aunt Hannah's taking us to the aquarium instead of Grandpa."

"Oh good. That will be more fun."

Olivia relayed all that information to Theodore.

The truck stopped next to Luke's rental car. Other than his car, the lot had a few other cars parked willy-nilly, avoiding the potholes.

"I doesn't look too busy tonight." Hannah slammed the truck door closed. "Let the fun begin."

Cal, being the gentleman that he was, held the pool hall's door open. Olivia shot through first and made a beeline to the bar. "Can I have a fizzy pink drink, Michael?"

"Sure thing. And how about your furry friend?" Michael placed a seltzer mixed with cranberry juice in front of Olivia.

"He can share mine if he gets thirsty."

Ruby carried Olivia's glass to a table away from the bar while Hannah talked to Michael.

He handed her an iced mug of Sam Adams beer. "On the house. I think you'll be needing this."

She took a long drink, leaving foam on her top lip. "And why is that?"

Michael leaned on the counter. "Meg called and told me you and your father are having some kind of showdown." His eyes moved to where Luke stood near the pool table with Olivia. "He was here Friday night with the woman who was murdered. It wasn't pretty."

Hannah's mouth scrunched to one side. "What do you mean? Did they argue?"

"It was more than an argument. She was wild—drunk, flirty, having a *good* time—and your dad stared at her like a shark on the prowl. Finally, she left with him. It was after midnight."

"Did you notice anything about the surfer guy, Moe? He and Adele were in some type of relationship."

Michael pulled his iPad from under the counter. "Look through the photos I took that night. See what you can find. I have to get the pizza going." He rolled his eyes. "Your father wants it to be served at seven, sharp. Does he ever relax and have a good time?"

"Ha. On his terms, but there's always an agenda."

"Oh, by the way, Meg told me to tell you to hold off on your pool game until she gets here."

"And?"

Michael held up his hands. "That's all I know."

Hannah quickly scanned through Michael's photos. She found plenty of Luke watching Adele and it gave her chills. He controlled his face well, but she knew there was fury behind his tense glare. She zoomed in on Adele and, sure enough, the mermaid necklace dangled around her neck. There were only a few photos with Moe, and he seemed to be watching both Adele and Karla.

"Hey, I could use some help." Ruby helped herself to Hannah's beer. "I'm out-numbered with you over here." She pulled Hannah's arm.

"Okay. I'm coming." She held her empty mug up toward Michael with two fingers raised.

Joanna stood at one end of the pool table. Luke had Olivia on a step-stool and showed her how to hold the cue stick. Together they hit the white ball to break the rest of the balls.

Olivia squealed in delight. "This is fun, Grandpa. Let's do it again."

Luke glanced at Hannah and winked. "Sure thing, Olivia. Hannah, rack them up again for us."

After several more breaks, Luke showed Olivia how to bank the ball and gave her a mini lesson in geometry which went right over her head.

"I'm hungry. Is the pizza ready?"

Right on time, Michael delivered two giant steamy pizzas. One with extra cheese and the other with pepperoni and onions. "Enjoy." He lowered his voice when he passed Hannah. "If possible."

Luke and Joanna sat on one side of the table; Hannah sat between Cal and Ruby on the other side. Olivia insisted on sitting at the end with Theodore in her lap.

"Are you feeling okay, Mom?" Hannah asked.

Joanna squeezed her forehead between her thumb and forefinger. "It feels like another migraine is coming on, but don't worry about me, I'll be fine."

Luke stood. "Let's get our game started before your mother needs to leave." He left his pizza, with one bite gone, on the table. "Unless you've changed your mind, Hannah." One thick white eyebrow raised in question and two steel gray eyes pierced into her unflinching stare.

"Of course not." She rubbed Great Aunt Caroline's ring for strength and again, like a lucky charm, the heat settled her jingling nerves.

"Good." He held her arm and led her to the pool table. "A friendly wager?"

She nodded. Every cell in her body tingled on high alert. This was it. Her dream on the line.

Luke leaned close. "Your property if I win."

"And you pay off *my* debt when I beat you." Hannah held his gaze, pleased that her response gave him a momentary pause before he managed a devious smile.

"Fat chance of that happening. Rack them up, honey. Or should I say, my-soon-to-be-homeless daughter. I'll even let you break."

Anger brewed in Hannah's gut. A fire that flamed into a determination she'd never known before. Some of the anger was at herself for being in this position. No one knew how big her debt had grown from upgrading the original cottages and snack bar to building her own new cottage. The bills had piled up faster than sand on a windy day. By winning this pool game, no one would have to know.

She smiled at her father, racked the balls, and took up her position for the break. She pointed her cue stick at the seven ball and the side pocket. "I'll call my usual shot." She chalked the cue and leaned over the table.

Before Hannah took her shot, the door of the Pub and Pool Hall opened.

Meg, Samantha, and Jack entered, followed by Pam in her police uniform.

Pam looked around the pool hall. "Don't let me interfere with your fun. I have enough time to chat with everyone in due course." She walked to the bar and in a voice loud enough for everyone to hear, she said, "Michael, I'd like to have a look at your photos from Friday night. I'm hoping they might clear up a small discrepancy about Adele Bailey."

Hannah watched her father.

Luke glanced at Joanna.

Joanna leaned on the table with her head in her hands and groaned. "Luke, I need to go back to the cottage to lie down. The pain is about to split my head open."

"I demand a rain check with this game, Hannah. I can't help when your mother gets a migraine."

Hannah leaned close to her father. "And I suppose you couldn't help your behavior Friday night and the displeasure with Adele's actions that Deputy Pam Larson will see in Michael's photos. Did you think Mom wouldn't find out?"

"You have no idea what you're talking about." Luke stormed from the pool hall with Joanna hanging on his arm.

CHAPTER 18

"You dodged a bullet, Hannah," Ruby said as Michael delivered another round of beers to their table. The tension in the pool hall followed Luke and Joanna out the door. The two sisters and Olivia were alone for the moment.

"Postponed, maybe, but this isn't over between me and Dad. You know how he never backs down. He wants my property and he's planning to get it one way or another."

"What did *you* put on the table if you won?" Ruby gave Olivia another slice of pizza.

Hannah filled her mouth with her own pizza to avoid answering Ruby's question. Did she want her sister to know the truth about her finances? But really, what difference did it make? She swallowed. "He has to pay off all my debt."

Ruby froze. "How much?"

Hannah sighed. "It built up faster than I realized with all the work Cal did for me to get the cottages updated and The Fishy Dish up to code. Great Aunt Caroline left me a slice of paradise but she hadn't maintained it well for many years."

"You should have told me. I would have helped with the money from Olivia's dad." Ruby covered Hannah's hand with her own.

"No, that money is for you and Olivia. I couldn't let you spend your nest egg on my business, but thanks for the thought." She choked up from Ruby's offer.

Ruby jabbed her sister with her elbow. "What is Pam finding in Michael's photos? You were looking at that iPad earlier, too."

"There are plenty of pictures of Dad watching Adele while they were here Friday night. He was angry, to say the least. And it shows that Adele still had her mermaid necklace."

"What does that all mean? Do you think Dad, you know..." Ruby glanced at Olivia who was busy trying to feed Theodore some pizza and didn't seem to be paying any attention to the conversation around her.

Suddenly, Olivia's head jerked up. "Can I go over with Cal?"

"Sure," Ruby said.

Hannah pursed her lips and pulled on the end of her braid. "It doesn't make sense. Adele was always his favorite of the three of us."

"But she wasn't his daughter. Maybe he held her to a different standard and when she didn't follow his *rules*, he lost it."

"That's possible, but it doesn't explain the necklace. How did Karla get it? Moe told me that he argued with Adele early Saturday morning and she threw it at him.

He could be the murderer. He also told me that he saw someone, maybe Karla, walking toward where he had just left Adele. If she was alive at that point, did Karla kill her and take the necklace for herself?"

"How will this ever get sorted out? Is she," Ruby tilted her head in Pam's direction, "making any progress?"

"Not that she shares with me, but my guess is that she knows a lot more than we know." Hannah pushed her plate away and groaned. "I shouldn't have had that last piece but it's so good. Maybe we should add pizza to The Fishy Dish menu."

Meg plopped down in the chair next to Hannah. "Did I hear you say you want to add pizza to the menu?"

"Yeah. What do you think?"

Meg's head bobbed one way, then the other, while she considered the question. "Actually, it's a good idea. It's a snack bar, after all, and everyone doesn't like fish dishes all the time. I could add one or two varieties and see what the response is."

Hannah smiled, glad that Meg gave a thumbs up to her idea. "Did you hear anything that Pam and Michael were talking about?"

Ruby said, "Hannah just filled me in on Moe and Karla's early Saturday morning travels and it sounds like they both had some interaction with Adele."

"Pam has them on her radar, but after looking at Michael's iPad I think she's got some more questions for your father." Meg's eyes shifted between Hannah and Ruby, gauging their reactions.

"I suspected that, and I'm wondering if that's why he made such a quick exit when Pam walked in. Karla told me he gave her a ride early Saturday morning which means they were both out and about."

"Up to no good, I suspect," Meg added. "Someone knows more than they are saying, or else there's a big fat lie leading Pam in the wrong direction."

"Aunt Hannah," Olivia called. "Come play pool with us. Cal isn't very good."

Hannah grinned. "That's good to know if I ever need to beat him at something," she said to Ruby. "I'm coming."

"Cal said you'd show me how to hit that one," she pointed to the eight ball, "into that pocket." Olivia pointed to the pocket at the opposite end of the table with a ball blocking the eight ball and another ball blocking the pocket.

Hannah's eyebrows jumped up. "He did, did he? I think a little wager should be on this shot."

"What's a wager?" Olivia asked, her face crunched into a frown.

"If I get that ball into that pocket like you pointed out, Cal has to do something nice for me. What do you think he should do?" Hannah tilted her head and looked at Olivia.

Olivia considered Cal, her face as serious as a six-year-old's could be. "He should take you out on his boat. Just the two of you. He told me he was going to surprise you with that sometime soon. It's a secret."

Hannah swallowed her laughter and didn't dare let her eyes meet Cal's, knowing full well they would both burst out laughing. "That's the perfect wager, and don't worry, I'll keep the secret."

"Wait a minute," Cal took hold of the cue stick. "If you *don't* get the ball in the pocket, I get a sleepover in your new cottage." His grin spread from ear to ear.

"A deal." Hannah stuck out her hand and they shook. She chalked her cue stick as she walked around the pool table. It certainly was a difficult shot but she had one path to the eight ball with the correct speed and two perfect banks. This was a test of her ability for when she had the rematch with her father. She told herself that if she made this shot, it meant she'd win the wager against him, too.

"Okay. I'm ready."

Olivia squealed.

Hannah put her finger to her lips. "Shhh. I have to concentrate."

Olivia covered her mouth with her hand. Her eyes grew wide with anticipation.

Hannah lined up her cue stick and sent the white ball bouncing from one side of the table to the other, headed toward the eight ball. She held her breath. The white ball tapped the eight ball with just enough force to send it on its way into the pocket. Hannah breathed and smiled. She still had the touch.

Olivia shrieked. "You did it. You did it, Aunt Hannah. Cal said you could, and now he has to take you out on his boat. Aren't you excited?"

Cal put his arm around Hannah's shoulder. "Are you?"

"Yes. You can't imagine." One eyebrow rose suggestively at his touch.

"It's not the surprise I hoped it would be, thanks to *someone* spoiling my secret, but watching Olivia's excitement balances it all out."

"Theodore," Olivia said to her teddy bear, "Hannah is the bestest at pool. No one can beat her."

Hannah didn't agree with Olivia, but there was only *one* person she needed to beat, not everyone. She had a lot riding on beating that one person, but her confidence after sinking that difficult shot rose significantly.

"I have a message for you." Jack stood next to Hannah. He pulled her to an empty table away from everyone else. "Nice shot, by the way."

"Good practice for a little wager I have with my father on a game of pool."

"How little?"

"He'll pay off all my debt when I beat him," Hannah said but she didn't meet Jack's eyes.

"And if he wins? As talented as you are, you have to consider that possibility."

"He gets my property."

"Caroline was afraid of something along those lines. You can't play that game. He'll figure out a way to beat you."

Hannah leaned close to Jack. Her voice came out barely above a whisper. "You don't understand. I can't make my next mortgage payment. I'll lose the property anyway if I don't get out from under the debt."

"No. Caroline will help. Trust her. Do not play that game of pool."

"We don't have a time set so I'll do my best to put him off." She sat back. "What's happening with the investigation? Is Pam getting any closer to finding the killer? My hope is that once the murder is solved, my parents will get back to what they love best—traveling the world."

Jack scooched his chair right up next to Hannah. "Rory is off the hook but no one knows the details. Moe, Karla, and your father are Pam's main suspects now, so there is a possibility that your father may not be doing too much traveling in his future."

"How did Rory get off? I heard he's home but I never talked to anyone that gave him an alibi. Karla said Rory dropped her off, then was going for a walk on the beach."

Jack nodded. "That was his plan but he went to a friend's house instead and Rory never took that walk on the beach."

"Huh," Hannah leaned an elbow on the table. "So why was he at the police station for so long?"

"The friend left Saturday morning for an overnight retreat—no phone, email, no outside communication of any kind—and Pam couldn't track him down until he came back to town this morning. His story checked out with what Rory said so he's got an airtight alibi."

"And the other three?"

"I hate to tell you this, but your father could be the killer."

Hannah felt Jack's eyes bore into her even though she was staring at the table. She had a lot of trouble believing it was possible. Adele meant too much to Luke. Even when it interfered with her own relationship with him all those years ago, he never pushed Adele away.

Adele's death did give Hannah a glimmer of hope that she and her father could work back to a better relationship. Over time. But not if he was the killer. Although, if he ended up in jail, that *would* solve the problem of Luke trying to maneuver the ocean front property away from her.

It was a classic no-win situation for her.

CHAPTER 19

Monday started out slowly, unlike the usual hectic pace of catching up after a busy weekend. Hannah took Nellie for a walk on the beach, hoping the peaceful routine would wash away her anxiety. It also gave her a chance to try to figure out a path back toward a better relationship with her father. She had always told herself she didn't care, but the truth was, when her father started to compare her to Adele all those years ago, she put up a wall around her heart to keep it from breaking. Now, she felt a small crack developing in that wall.

Was their relationship beyond repair? How could she make him understand that Great Aunt Caroline's legacy was *her* responsibility and it shouldn't interfere in his life?

Without thinking, her feet followed the familiar path from the beach to Jack's house. She laughed when she opened his front door and heard his smoke alarm shrieking its ear-piercing warning that Jack was burning toast. Again. The charred smell hit her nose seconds later.

Muttering came from the kitchen. "Come on in. I made extra coffee expecting you to barge in on my peace and quiet."

Hannah dismantled the smoke alarm and leaned against the door leading into the kitchen. "You call this peace and quiet? I'd hate to be here when you have a real emergency."

"Make yourself useful and get out a couple of mugs for the coffee. I suppose you want some eggs with your toast?"

Jack's morning grumpiness comforted Hannah in a way she couldn't explain. Maybe it was the predictability of his morning routine and how he welcomed her into it, or maybe it was merely the fact that he accepted her for who she was.

That was always the hurdle with her father. He wanted Hannah to be who *he* thought she should be. She sighed.

"What's all the doom and gloom sighing for? It's a new day. You may as well start it on a high note before the disasters start to pile up." He put two plates with eggs and toast on the table and held a dog bone out for Nellie, who very politely took it without leaving any slobber on Jack's fingers. Hannah sat and poured the coffee. "With some luck, this gourmet breakfast won't be the high note of your day, but if it is, well...I'll leave it at that. Dig in while it's hot."

Hannah chuckled. "If I stick my head in a sand dune after I eat, I think I could call Monday a success."

Jack dug into the scrambled eggs. "You know my secret?"

Hannah's ears perked up. "To life's problems?"

"To perfect scrambled eggs. I add a teaspoon or two of olive oil. It makes them super creamy. But since you brought up the secret of life, I'll give you some free advice that's helped me reach the ripe old age of eighty-one."

Hannah sipped her coffee. She closed her eyes and let Jack's delicious blend do its magic—calm and sooth—until the jolt of caffeine spread through her veins.

"Don't overthink everything, Hannah. Sometimes, you have to give yourself permission to just act on what you know is the right thing to do."

Her eyes popped open. "Does this advice have anything to do with the bet I have on the table with my father?" She heard a flicker of annoyance in her words.

"The fact that you asked that question must tell you something. It's not what *I* think you should or shouldn't do. You have to figure that out for yourself. But don't make a rash decision based on your emotions. What decision can you live with if the outcome isn't what you hope for? Once you start down a path, you can't control where it will end. I learned that lesson the hard way."

Hannah knew Jack was right. And she knew she couldn't live with herself if she lost Great Aunt Caroline's legacy to her father in a moment of panic during a pool game. She wasn't a gambler. What had she been thinking when she accepted his challenge?

"Your father is playing with your emotions and he knows it. Do you know what I think?"

Hannah lifted her eyes to meet Jack's.

"With the speed he left the Pub and Pool Hall last night, I think he's considering the possibility that he might lose to you. If he does, it represents much more than just losing a game of pool. To someone like your father, it might mean that he cuts you loose forever. Is that what you want?"

Hannah's head was spinning from this conversation. No, it wasn't what she wanted. She wanted to leave a door open. "I have to work harder to keep the property because it's my future. And it's the right thing to do to honor Great Aunt Caroline's trust in me." She shoveled a forkful of eggs into her mouth. "These are the best eggs I've ever had."

Jack chuckled and mumbled loud enough for Hannah to hear. "That's because you've made the right decision."

With her stomach full, her anxiety settled down, and Nellie at her side, Hannah decided to take the beach route back to her cottage. Another dose of hearing the waves' rhythmic crashing on the beach and the seagulls calling overhead might be the tonic to face the rest of the day.

Heavy breathing made Hannah turn around.

Nellie woofed and ran toward the runner approaching quickly.

Karla caught up to Hannah and jogged in place until her breathing slowed and she matched her pace to Hannah's.

"Do you always run on the beach?" Hannah asked.

"Usually. But I've changed my route. I was running Saturday morning when I found Adele's body and I don't want to go that way anymore so I've been coming in this direction instead."

"That must have been quite a shock for you." Hannah chose her words carefully with the hope that she could pry more details from Karla.

Karla quickly wiped her cheek with the back of her hand. "It was a terrible shock. Especially after all the arguing the night before."

Hannah nodded but remained silent, giving Karla room to continue her train of thought.

"I hate to admit it, but my first thought was that Rory killed her. He told me he was going to walk on the beach and I saw his shovel next to Adele's body and I know he was devastated that he didn't win." Her words rushed out. "I think I even said all that to Deputy Larson when she showed up. I just babbled away and I think it's all my fault that Rory ended up at the police station all weekend."

"But he's home now. Do you know the details? Why he was released?" Hannah wasn't planning to offer what she knew about Rory's alibi.

Karla laughed, a nervous giggle. "He was at a friend's house when Adele was killed. I should have thought of that but my mind only went in one direction. And when I couldn't find him Saturday morning, it made him look even guiltier."

"When you couldn't find him after you found Adele's body?"

"Even before. I couldn't sleep and went looking for him. Remember? I told you your father gave me a ride."

"Yes. You did tell me that. When did Moe show up?"

"He just appeared, almost like he had been nearby, waiting for someone."

"Maybe he was waiting for Adele?"

Karla shrugged. "At the time, I didn't really think about it. He was just there and took charge of calling the police since I couldn't function." She stopped walking. "He has a habit of showing up at odd times."

"Did Moe tell you he and Adele had an argument early Saturday morning on the beach?"

Karla shook her head.

Hannah touched Karla's arm. "When did he give you the mermaid necklace?"

Karla shivered. "I can't believe he re-gifted that jewelry; and from his dead ex-girlfriend. There has to be something wrong with him."

"But when did he give it to you?"

"Why? What difference does it make?" An edge of anger crept into Karla's voice.

"To be honest, I'm not sure if Adele gave it to him or he took it from her."

Karla picked up the pace, almost as if she was trying to get away from Hannah.

Hannah held her arm. "It's important, Karla. When did Moe give you the necklace?"

"I lied. He didn't give it to me. I found it in the sand when I found her body. I showed it to Moe and he told me to say he gave it to me. All right? Are you happy? Now, I feel like I'm ruining someone else's life." She bolted into a run, leaving Hannah and Nellie alone on the beach.

Moe Meyer lied.

What was he trying to cover up?

Was he afraid someone saw him on the beach and he needed the necklace story to prove Adele had been alive when he argued with her? Not that it proved anything in the long run. So why did he need Karla to lie for him?

All the peacefulness of her beach walk blew away with the salty ocean breeze when Hannah saw her parents sitting at one of the picnic tables in front of The Fishy Dish.

CHAPTER 20

"Sorry we left so suddenly last night," Joanna said as soon as Hannah was close to her parents. "My migraine hit me like a tidal wave; I thought I was going to be sick to my stomach."

"How is it now?" Hannah asked.

"A good night's sleep in your lovely cottage was all I needed." She reached her hand out to pat Nellie. "When did you get your dog? She's lovely."

"Nellie sort of came with everything else." Nellie woofed when she heard her name. "She's been a wonderful companion in many ways."

"You finally got a dog," Luke stated. "Something you always wanted, but not something that works well when you travel a lot."

Hannah sat across from her parents. "And that's not a problem for me, is it? I'm happy here. I don't have any travel plans. Nellie keeps me company and is Olivia's best friend."

Luke frowned. "Ruby is raising that girl all wrong. She talks to a teddy bear, and now you say her best friend is a dog?"

Hannah ignored his comments. She had to choose her battles wisely and not get sucked into every challenge he made.

Joanna stood. She ran her fingers over Hannah's hair. "I'll leave the two of you to catch up while I start packing."

Hannah raised her eyebrows. "You're planning to leave?" she asked her father.

"Not today. That police officer said we need to stay here until she's done with her investigation. But, yes, we are planning to head back to California. In case you hadn't noticed, your mother isn't happy here."

"The stress of your visit here can't help." Hannah avoided mentioning Adele by name, but she was certain her father understood her meaning.

Something in his expression changed. He looked old for the first time Hannah could remember. And sad.

"Joanna had such high hopes for this trip—to spend time with you, Ruby, and Olivia. She never understood the problem between you and Adele until this trip. That ruined everything for her." Luke talked while his eyes scanned the horizon.

"But you always understood, didn't you Dad? How Adele came between you and me. But it didn't bother you." Hannah felt her morning coffee try to make an exit the wrong way.

Luke didn't respond at first. "I thought the competition between you and Adele would make you stronger. Tougher. Help you to take charge of yourself instead of being pushed around by others. And she needed a good, steady, grounding role model."

His last comment surprised Hannah but there was no way a tiny sort-of compliment would cancel out the years of criticism. "It made me resist being pushed around by *you*. And that's what all this is about." Hannah swept her arm to encompass her buildings, the beach, and the ocean. "I finally found what I love." She placed her hand gently over his. "I don't expect you to understand, but I hope you accept my choice."

He nodded and rose from the table. "Don't forget that game of pool. I won't leave until we settle that wager. Now, I'd better check on your mother."

So much for hoping he was beginning to understand her. "Before you go, I need to ask you something."

Luke paused.

"What were you doing driving around early Saturday morning? Karla told me you gave her a ride, so don't try to deny it. And I saw you rushing from the parking lot back to your cottage."

He clenched his jaw. "Looking for something."

"Did you find it?"

"I found one thing and lost something else."

His shoulders sagged but he turned and left, leaving Hannah to wonder what he found and what he lost. Whatever it was, she had a bad feeling in the pit of her stomach about his comment. It sounded like a riddle, and the fact that he still wanted to play that game of pool unsettled her.

Cal joined Hannah at the picnic table with two coffees. He slid one toward Hannah. "You look distracted."

She picked it up but didn't drink. "I probably don't need any more yet. I had some of Jack's coffee this morning."

"In that case," Cal took the cup back, "I'll drink them both while you tell me about your conversation with your father. He had the look of someone who lost his best friend."

"Maybe he did. Maybe Adele was his best friend but something happened between them that he is hiding."

Cal pulled Hannah's arm, forcing her to stand. "You need a change of scenery so let's finish moving you into your new cottage."

"You call that a change of scenery? I thought you meant you were taking me out on that boat trip that I won last night. Oops." Hannah covered her mouth and tried not to laugh. "I forgot that Olivia said it was a secret."

"I should know better than to trust a six-year-old with a secret. Especially when it involves her favorite aunt."

"Um, I'm her only aunt so the bar is pretty low.

"Well, you can feel good that you beat Theodore out by a hair for first place in her world."

"My competition is a teddy bear?" Hannah tried to slap Cal but he sprinted away. When she caught him at the door of her cottage, he pulled her inside and held her close. "Don't worry, you don't have any competition for number one in *my* world."

She let herself relax and enjoy his strong arms around her. Cal was her rock when times got tough, and right about now, there were too many loose ends that she couldn't ignore.

She pulled away. "There's not too much left here to carry to my new cottage, and if we're quick, we should be done in time for me to get to The Fishy Dish to help Meg and Samantha with the lunch rush."

They each grabbed a box of packed-up kitchen stuff and trudged up the hill. The sight of her new cottage made Hannah smile. She had to find the time to unpack and move in properly so Samantha could move into her old space. Hannah brought the boxes inside to unpack. Cal volunteered to be the pack mule, lugging everything else up from her old cottage.

She pulled a ceramic casserole dish from the box and rubbed her fingers over the smooth blue surface. It had belonged to her mother but Joanna passed it on to Hannah when she got her first apartment. The memories of cooking with her mother brought a tear to her eye.

Footsteps banged across her porch.

Nellie's nails clacked over the hardwood floor toward the front door.

Hannah stood on her tippy toes and slid the dish into a cupboard. "Do you have more kitchen stuff?"

"I'm not sure what Cal dumped in my arms."

Hannah twisted around, surprised to hear her mother's voice instead of Cal's. "Oh. You don't have to carry stuff up."

Joanna ignored Hannah's comment. "Your father went for a walk and I want to talk to you without him listening to our conversation." She put the box on Hannah's kitchen counter. "I asked Cal to give us a few minutes alone. I hope that's okay?"

Hannah nodded. It wasn't like she had a choice at this point anyway. Her mother stood before her, obviously waiting to get something off her chest.

Joanna put her iPad on the small kitchen table in front of Hannah. "I brought this along for you."

Hannah pulled two chairs closer to the table and waited for her mother to sit. Her stomach twisted into a knot of anticipation. Joanna was more the let's-pretend-everything-is-okay type of person but

Hannah suspected this conversation was going in an, it's-time-we-air-out-the-problems direction.

Joanna cleared her throat. She folded her hands on the table in front of her. "I'm worried about your father."

"What do you mean, Mom?" Hannah kept her face calm even though her insides felt like a worm wiggling on a hook.

A big sigh escaped through her lips and her body sagged. "I had such high hopes for this visit. You know, hang out with my girls, but it turned into a disaster around Adele. There, I said her name. Adele. She ruined everything in our family, didn't she?"

"Is that what you think?" Of course Hannah agreed with her mother, but she wanted to hear what else Joanna thought about the situation. She was more than shocked to hear this sentiment from her mother after so many years of silence about the situation. Was Luke the only one who had been blinded by Adele's manipulations?

Joanna shifted in her chair. She ran her fingers through her long hair. In some ways, at least on the surface, when Hannah looked at her mother, she saw an older version of herself. The similarities ended once she looked beyond their brown eyes, creamy skin, and long hair. Joanna had always cow-towed to Luke's needs and Hannah insisted on being her own person.

"Yes. Adele, in her needy way, became your father's project. And he can never let go of a project until it's complete."

"That doesn't make sense," Hannah said with disgust dripping from her words. "Adele always needed more and more. She became a never-ending project."

"That *was* the problem." Joanna stood and looked out the window. "This is a fantastic view. I understand why you love it here. I think your father is jealous of you, Hannah."

"Jealous? He should be proud of me and supportive, not envious and plotting to steal something I love."

"One hurdle is gone." Joanna turned around quickly. "Do you think you and your father can mend those fences now?"

Hannah shrugged. "It's up to him. He still wants to play that game of pool, but if we play, it will destroy one of us, won't it?" She opened her mother's iPad and hit the photo icon.

"I mean, look at these photos. They're all of Adele. "Her finger moved the photos across the screen. "You haven't even taken one photo of me or Ruby or Olivia. Adele posing with her mermaid sculpture. Adele out to dinner with the two of you. Adele—"

Joanna grabbed the iPad from Hannah. "That's not true." She stared at the screen and searched through the photos herself. "Luke must have deleted all the photos of you girls." Anguish laced her words. Fire burned in her eyes.

Joanna rushed from Hannah's cottage.

"Where are you going, Mom?"

The door slammed closed behind Joanna, sending a blow straight to Hannah's heart.

Luke destroyed everyone with his selfish needs.

CHAPTER 21

Cal quietly returned to Hannah's cottage with another armful of boxes. "This is about it from your cottage, but," he placed Joanna's iPad on the table, "I found this on the path. Your mother must have dropped it when she raced out of here."

Hannah didn't move from the spot in front of her window. Joanna was barely visible but she couldn't take her eyes away until her mother's slim body disappeared from view. Why would her father erase photos from the iPad? Was there something he didn't want anyone to see?

Their visit managed to turn into a bigger disaster than she ever imagined. When Ruby waved the postcard in her face Friday morning, all she expected was an awkward and emotional visit, but now she was trying to solve a murder, save her business, and protect her niece. And her father's behavior was suspicious at best and scary at worst if she let herself consider the possibilities of his involvement in any of her problems.

"Your mother asked me to stay away so she could talk to you," Cal said. He lightly placed his hand on the small of her back. "What happened?"

How was Hannah supposed to explain her emotional turmoil? It was all too raw to put into words. "We talked about Adele. Of course. Even with her dead, she still has managed to dominate my family." Hannah sighed deeply. "I have to see how today is shaping up in The Fishy Dish."

She picked up the iPad and shoved it in one of her kitchen drawers. She'd study it later when she could be more objective. Maybe. Not that she wanted to see all the photos of Adele again.

Cal, Hannah, and Nellie walked down the path together. "I'll make sure all the tables and umbrellas are set up, and rake the sand." They split apart at the back door of the kitchen, Cal heading toward the tables with Nellie and Hannah entering the kitchen.

Meg's head whipped around. She looked like she was about to explode with excitement. "I've been sitting on pins and needles waiting for you to get here. I've got some news."

Samantha stopped chopping the cabbage for coleslaw. "And you didn't share it with me already?"

"Hannah needs to hear it." Meg leaned on the center island. "You know how Rory's friend showed up and gave him an alibi?"

Hannah nodded. "Yeah, Rory dropped Karla off before he went to his friend's house and didn't take a walk on the beach like he planned."

"But he might have taken that walk after all." Meg crossed her arms with a you-won't-believe-it expression on her face.

"The friend lied?" Samantha blurted out.

"Not exactly. Rory did go to the friend's house, but the friend wasn't there the whole time," Meg explained.

"*He* went to the beach?" Hannah asked.

"No, nothing like that. Rory's friend went to the Pub and Pool Hall. Michael fixed the lights in his sign on Friday, but they were out again by Saturday morning and he fixed them a *second* time on Saturday. But he never got around to checking his surveillance video until this morning to find out who broke them. He called to tell me who climbed on the roof early Saturday morning around four and busted the lights. Michael figures he had to be away from his house for at least an hour." She paused with a smile starting at the corners of her mouth. "The person on the video tape was Rory's friend."

"Was Rory with him? If they were together, he'd still have an alibi," Hannah said.

Meg shook her head. "No one else was with him on the roof or in the car."

"Odd. Why'd he do it then if he wasn't showing off for his buddies?"

"Michael already confronted him with the information and said he wouldn't call the police if he confessed and told him why he did it. It was a dumb dare and he thought early in the morning was the safest time to go. Obviously, he didn't know about the camera."

Hannah pulled on her braid. "Michael has to tell the police. This potentially gives Rory a chance to be at the scene of the crime."

"Michael didn't know this kid was Rory's alibi. He will turn over the tape if he has to, but he wants you to talk to Rory first. Find out what you can with the threat of revealing the tape to get him to talk."

"Okay. If Rory did lie, he'd better have a good explanation." Hannah had her apron off and was out the door and in her car with her mind racing through all the possibilities. Was she wrong about Rory all along being the murderer? Why else would he lie about being on the beach? If he was.

It didn't take Hannah long to drive into town and park on Main Street. She took a deep breath, rubbed Great Aunt Caroline's ring for strength, and slid out of her car.

She looked up at the window of Rory's apartment window that faced the street and saw a flicker of a shadow and the curtain falling back into place. Someone was definitely inside.

She took the steps two at a time and knocked on his door. "Rory? It's Hannah. I need to talk to you."

Silence met her words. She jiggled the door and it turned. Should she go in?

She licked her lips and tightened her muscles.

She pushed the door open and peeked inside.

Rory sat at his kitchen table working on a lobster sculpture.

"Can I come in, Rory?" Hannah forced her voice to sound calm and friendly.

"Sure. I'm in the middle of something, though. But have a seat if you want."

Hannah stood just inside the door. She felt safer staying close to an exit in case she needed to make a hasty retreat. "Is anyone else here with you?"

"Nope, just me and my sculptures."

Hannah watched as Rory chiseled a piece of the wood he was working with.

"I saw your other pieces of art," Hannah gestured toward his living room. "You're extremely talented."

He shrugged. "I guess the judges didn't think so, did they?" He finally lifted his eyes to meet Hannah's gaze. "My sand sculpture was much more intricate and complicated than the mermaid." He shrugged again. "Win some, lose some."

"I'm glad you're friend returned to confirm your alibi. A lot of people were worried about you."

Rory picked up his knife and began to whittle a delicate part of the claw.

Hannah felt beads of sweat drip down her side inside her t-shirt. "Your friend wasn't at his house for the whole night, though, was he?"

Rory's knife slipped. "What are you talking about?"

"And someone saw you on the beach early Saturday morning." The momentary look of panic in his eyes confirmed what Hannah suspected when she told her lie.

Rory set his knife down next to the chisel. He ran both hands through his hair, making it stand out in all directions. He pushed himself up from his chair.

Hannah held her ground but reached behind herself to keep one hand on the doorknob.

"You're right. I did go to the beach, but Adele was already dead when I found her."

This turn of events wasn't what Hannah expected to hear. So far, anyone who admitted to being on the beach said Adele was still alive. "Why all the silence then? Why didn't you go straight to the police?"

"I couldn't admit to being there. When I saw my shovel lying next to the body and blood still dripping from her head wound, my life flashed before my eyes and I knew exactly what it would look like to everyone. I lost to her. I argued with her. How convenient that I found her body with my shovel next to her bloody head." He shoved his hands into the pockets of his shorts. "And I was right. Deputy Larson took me to jail and I thought I'd never get out again."

"Until your friend returned and lied for you."

Rory nodded.

Hannah moved toward Rory. "You have to tell the truth before the video is turned over to the police showing your friend at the Pub and Pool Hall leaving you alone at the time Adele was murdered. Removing your alibi."

Rory shook his head. "I can't do that. I'll go back to jail if I have to."

"Who are you protecting, Rory? Is it Karla?"

Rory's jaw tightened. "We have a signal if I need to talk to her when she's home. She has a string hanging out her window that I pull and a little bell rings. I went straight to her house when I found Adele but Karla wasn't home. I needed to talk to her."

"Or were you checking for another reason? Maybe you suspected Karla killed Adele. Did you see her on the beach after you found Adele? Karla told me she was out looking for you."

"I saw someone running away. I didn't want to believe it was Karla, but in my gut I was sure it was. She loves to run on the beach and the moonlight glistened on her hair. She had her heart set on me winning so we could get out of Hooks Harbor. She cared more than I did but I wanted to win for her."

"And she told you she would leave you if you didn't win, didn't she?" Hannah pushed Rory as gently as possible.

Rory's whole body sagged. "I love her. Everything I cared about was crashing down."

"You can't protect her if she's the murderer. You have to tell the truth."

"I don't know the truth. I don't know if it was Karla. I don't know if whoever it was, was even the murderer." He sat in his chair with his head resting in his hands. "I don't know what to do."

"How about you tell Deputy Larson what you just told me before she discovers for herself that you lied about being with your friend at his house for the whole. That will look bad for you. You don't have to say you saw Karla since you don't know if it was her. Just tell the truth."

"No. Not yet. I want to talk to Karla first and find out what her truth is."

"Karla made plans to go to Florida with Moe when you were in jail. They almost left until Moe got picked up for questioning." Hannah hated to hit Rory with this betrayal by his girlfriend, but if he was protecting Karla, he needed to know exactly what her intentions were.

His eyes narrowed into angry slits. "I don't believe you."

Hannah saw a tear run down his cheek before he swiped it away with the back of his hand.

"Be careful who you decide to protect, Rory." And, of course, there's always the possibility that you are trying to protect yourself, she added silently.

CHAPTER 22

Hannah called Jack as soon as she got in her car. She didn't want to believe that Rory killed Adele, but she couldn't ignore the possibility. If he *was* lying, he sure was convincing. And if he wasn't? Then Karla better have one heck of a good explanation for being on the beach.

"Jack, I'm not sure what to do with this information," she began when he answered his phone. "Rory had a window of unmonitored time while he was at his friend's house. He could have gone to the beach early Saturday morning."

"I know. Meg already told me about Michael's video."

"I just left Rory's apartment. He admitted to me that he went to the beach and said Adele was already dead when he found her."

Hannah heard Jack breathing for several seconds before he responded. "So, he *did* go to the beach."

She shifted her phone to her left hand and started her car. "I think you need to call Pam and fill her in before Rory does something stupid."

"You think he might run away?"

"I don't think so, not without Karla. I don't know where she is. But he may have been lying to me the whole time, too." Hannah pulled into the street. "I'm heading back to my place. Meet me there."

"Hannah?" Jack's voice sounded odd. "Your mother took Olivia for a walk down the beach and they haven't come back yet. Ruby's in a panic."

Her fingers tightened like a vise on the steering wheel. "I'm on my way."

Joanna with Olivia? At least it wasn't Luke. Where was *he*? Hannah made herself focus. She counted the telephone poles as she went by to keep her mind in neutral.

Her father's rental car was conspicuously absent from the parking lot when Hannah arrived. She ran to the snack bar in a panic.

Samantha pointed down the beach. "Ruby just went in that direction. Maybe we should look the other way."

Hannah called Nellie and crouched in front of the retriever and stared into her milk-chocolate eyes. "Where's Olivia?" she pleaded, hoping that Nellie understood her. "This is the time to use your nose."

Nellie woofed and wagged her tail. She trotted in the direction toward the marina. "Okay, we'll head this way. If Ruby returns, tell her to stay here," Hannah called to Meg.

"Wait a minute, I'm coming with you," Samantha said. She pulled on her sun hat and tied it under her chin. "I'm tired of missing out on all the excitement."

Hannah glared at her.

Samantha held Hannah's arm. "You know what I mean. I can't sit on my fingers any longer and wait to be filled in on the information. I need to help."

Hannah nodded. "Fair enough. More eyes can't hurt." Hannah's feet flew over the hot sand as Nellie trotted ahead.

"Plus I had a chat with your father. I thought I could fill you in while we're walking."

A groan escaped through Hannah's lips. "Please don't tell me there's more drama from him. I should be looking for Karla instead of worrying about Olivia and my mother."

"Karla?"

"I just came from Rory's apartment and he said he thinks he saw her on the beach. After he saw Adele's body. He's been covering for her; afraid she killed Adele," Hannah explained.

"That ties in with what your father told me. He gave Karla a ride early Saturday morning. He said she kept wiping her hands on her pants."

"Wait a minute. Start at the beginning. Why were you even talking to my father?" Hannah watched

Nellie follow a scent to the water's edge, then back up to drier sand. She imagined Olivia darting to the water, squealing with delight when the wave splashed her toes, and retreating. Maybe Nellie really was on her trail.

"Don't get mad at me, but I saw your mother head up to your new cottage and I decided to pretend I needed to clean their cottage. So I knocked on the door with a pile of clean towels. Your dad came out. I said good morning and how was he doing, blah, blah, blah. You know, just some friendly chit chat."

"You certainly have a knack for that. And did he fall for your come-on?"

Samantha looked at Hannah over the top of her sunglasses. "Of course. Samantha Featherstone doesn't take no for an answer, dear. I had your father eating out of my hand before he even had a chance to sit down and enjoy the view from the porch of *Something's Fishy.*"

"When you tell it like that, I actually have a tiny," Hannah held her fingers up about a hair's width apart, "bit of sympathy for him."

"Anyway, he asked Karla what was on her hands and she kind of hemmed and hawed and never answered. He gave her his handkerchief to use, which she stuck in her bag when she was done."

"Possible evidence. If we can find it."

"Exactly." Samantha beamed with pride.

"Or he wiped his own hands and planted it on Karla and told you she used it," Hannah suggested. "Everyone is pointing their finger at someone else so it's impossible to separate the truth from the lies."

"I didn't think of that." Samantha's proud grin turned upside down into a frustrated frown.

Suddenly, Nellie streaked straight down the beach. Relief flooded through Hannah. Olivia's delighted screech when she saw Nellie was music to Hannah's ears.

"The search and rescue dog," Joanna said matter-of-factly when Hannah stood in front of her, casting her mother in a shadow.

"Ruby was worried, Mom. You can't just disappear with a six-year-old and not expect people to look for her."

"She's my granddaughter, for crying out loud, Hannah. What did you think I was planning to do?"

Several comments flew through Hannah's mind but it was pointless to let the conversation continue. Olivia was safe and that was all that mattered at this point. The fact that Hannah even considered that her mother might harm Olivia disturbed her.

Hannah sent a text to Ruby telling her the news and that they'd be back soon.

Ruby responded with a smiley face with hearts for eyes.

Joanna remained sitting in the sand, gazing at the horizon. "We never should have come," she said, more to herself than to Hannah. "Adele managed to ruin everything. I don't know if your father will ever forgive me."

"What are you talking about? Forgive you for what?"

"For coming here." She flicked her wrist dismissively. "It's not your problem." Joanna pushed her hand in the sand and stood. "Shall we walk back now, Olivia?"

Olivia was already well on her way back to The Fishy Dish with Samantha holding her hand and Nellie glued to her side. Samantha reached down and picked up something that she showed to Olivia. Nellie stuck her nose in, too, and sniffed. Olivia tucked whatever it was in her pocket, most likely to be forgotten until Ruby found the treasure sometime in the future.

"Wait, Mom. Dad went to the beach early Saturday morning, didn't he?" Hannah asked as she and her mother walked side by side.

"Yes, he did. But it's not what you think. He only wanted to keep an eye on Adele. She was drunk and he was worried she might walk into the ocean and drown."

"That's what he told you?"

"Yes. He always tried to protect her." She shrugged. "But this time he couldn't."

"Mom?" Hannah waited for her mother to look at her. "Do you think Dad killed Adele?"

Joanna burst out laughing. "Are you kidding me? Your father would kill himself before he could harm one hair on Adele's head. Sure, he got angry with her at times, but he always tried to keep her safe." She linked her arm with Hannah's. "This is nice, walking with you and not worrying that Adele will stick her needs between us."

Hannah sighed with relief. The thought of her father being a murderer had festered in the back of her brain. She pushed the thought down and refused to take it seriously now. With her mothers' reaction, the worry was all but gone. Either Moe, Karla, or possibly Rory must be the murderer.

It had to be one of them.

Maybe the handkerchief that Hannah's father gave Karla could solve the mystery.

Or confuse everything further.

CHAPTER 23

Hannah was content to sit at the counter of The Fishy Dish and have lunch with Olivia. It was a simple, uncomplicated activity. Joanna, saying she was tired, had returned to her cottage but Hannah suspected she wanted to avoid answering any more questions.

Olivia dipped a French fry in ketchup, licked off the ketchup, and dipped it again.

"You'll run out of ketchup before your fries are gone if you keep dipping and never eating," Hannah said.

Olivia snuck a soggy French fry to Nellie. "They're disappearing, Aunt Hannah."

Hannah turned her head so Olivia couldn't see her laughing.

"Can I have some more ketchup? I like a puddle on my plate."

Hannah squeezed another big blob on Olivia's plate. "Eat some of your fish sandwich, too. Meg made it special, just the way you like it with extra tartar sauce."

Olivia took a big bite. "It's yummy, but I'm getting full." She patted her stomach. "Can I have ice cream?"

Hannah looked at Ruby and rolled her eyes. "That's your call. Did she eat enough yet?"

Ruby cut the fish sandwich in half. "Finish this and then you can have a *small* dish of ice cream."

Hannah swung her feet and chomped on her sandwich while Hannah told Ruby about her conversation with their mother.

"So who could it be?" Ruby asked, referring to who killed Adele.

"If Moe told me the truth and Adele was still alive after he argued with her, he said he saw a woman near the marina. Possibly Karla. Rory finally admitted that he was also at the beach but Adele was already dead and he saw a woman running away. Again, it sounds like Karla could be guilty and Rory is protecting her. And Dad picked Karla up and gave her a ride to Rory's apartment. She was wiping something off her hands." Saying it all out loud certainly didn't paint a pretty picture for Karla.

"Did you tell Jack all this? He's the one who pulled you into the investigation to begin with. He's not going to be happy with this information since Karla's grandmother is his new special lady friend."

Hannah leaned both elbows on the counter. She knew Ruby was right but she didn't want to have the conversation about Karla with Jack. She snuck a couple of French fries from Olivia's plate while Olivia was occupied sneaking fries to Nellie.

"Don't let Meg see her feeding those special hand-cut fries to the dog. It won't go over well at all," Ruby said.

"Meg will be okay with *Nellie* getting the fries. She's not just *any* dog, you know." Hannah silently thanked her Great Aunt Caroline for having the foresight of sending Nellie to her right after she moved in.

"Good point. It's amazing how she keeps her eyes on Olivia, making my job easier." Ruby polished the counter with gusto. "Don't look now, but Dad is heading in this direction. He looks like he swallowed a nasty pill."

Hannah immediately looked over her shoulder. How can you not look when someone says *don't look*, she told herself. In Hannah's opinion, Ruby had actually described her father's face much too kindly. Hannah decided a more apt description would be the panicked expression of someone choking on a sharp fish bone.

"*Hannah*. We need to talk."

So much for the possibility of a crack in the wall she'd built to protect herself from him. With a voice *demanding* her attention instead of requesting it, the crack sealed before Hannah could blink twice.

She faced Luke. "About what?"

"Your mother. What did you talk about? She's terribly upset."

Hannah slid off the bar stool. "Let's talk in my office."

She led the way, opened the door, and waited for Luke to walk in first. He headed toward her swivel chair behind the desk, but Hannah stopped him. "You can sit here." She pointed to a chair opposite her desk. She had no intention of letting him have the seat of power.

Hannah maneuvered around the big oak desk that had belonged to Great Aunt Caroline. She rubbed the ring on her finger and felt a tingle of warmth spread up her finger. It was probably friction from her vigorous rubbing but it was soothing, none the less.

She sat and folded her hands together in front of herself. "Okay. What's going on?"

"Joanna is packing and said we have to leave. Now. She thinks you don't want us here." Luke cocked his head and challenged Hannah with his piercing stare.

"First of all, I was under the impression you aren't supposed to leave until Adele's murder is solved. After all, you may have been the last person to see her alive."

"You know that isn't true. The last person to see Adele alive would be the murderer."

"Exactly. And Mom said you went to the beach early Saturday morning. Did you see Adele? Alive?" Hannah kept her eyes on her father's face. He was an expert at hiding his emotions but, if he slipped, Hannah didn't want to miss anything.

He flinched. His voice dropped. "She was already dead. Lying in the sand as if she was star-gazing. I couldn't do anything to help her so I went back to my car."

"And gave Karla a ride?"

He nodded. "She was agitated, said she was out looking for her boyfriend. She told me he had planned to take a walk on the beach."

"So, that's why you assumed Rory killed Adele? Because someone said something about someone else's actions? That story has a lot of holes in it."

"I know, but I wanted someone to blame." He ran his hand over his face in his only show of vulnerability.

"Besides yourself? That's what I asked Mom—if she thought *you* killed Adele."

Luke's eyebrows shot up. "What did she say?"

Hannah moved a letter-opener back and forth under her hand. She pointed it at her father. "Let's make sure your stories are straight and you tell *me* what she said."

"Joanna told you that I was trying to protect Adele but I failed." Luke rubbed his hands on his pants. "It's hard for me to admit that fact. If she said something different, she lied." Luke blinked several times.

Hannah had never seen so much emotion etched in his face.

"Why would she lie? Mom has nothing to hide."

Luke looked away. "She has done a good job all these years."

Hannah's mind flashed back to snippets of her mother's comments about Adele ruining their lives. Was that what he was referring to?

As if Luke could read Hannah's mind, he continued, "She resented all the time I spent with Adele. She was convinced that was why you and I didn't get along." He looked out the window toward the beach. "I thought she was wrong. All Joanna wanted was for you and Ruby to be happy. For the four of us to be happy. What I never admitted to myself was how Adele manipulated me against you."

"Because you loved the attention she gave you. She knew how to flatter you, tell you what you wanted to hear and exaggerate all that I did wrong." Hannah should have been pleased to finally have her father understand how Adele had lied to control him, but in reality, it was sad to see him deflated from hearing the truth. "And what did *you* want, Dad?"

He rubbed his neck with a pained expression. "I made a promise to Adele's father, my best friend, to keep an eye on her. He knew he wasn't going to beat the cancer that spread through his body. Adele pushed all the boundaries but I made a promise and needed to honor it. I always thought you would be fine—that you didn't need me as much as Adele did." He looked at Hannah. "I was wrong, wasn't I?"

"You never told us about that promise. I always considered Adele my competition for your attention."

Luke shifted in the chair, obviously miserable.

"Mom told me you would never forgive her."

"For what?" His brow furrowed.

"For coming here, she said, but I think she meant something more."

"Maybe she did." Luke stood. "We will be leaving soon." And just like that, the conversation ended and he left Hannah's office.

Cal knocked lightly on the door. "Busy?"

Hannah waved him inside.

"Were you near the marina recently?"

"No. Why?"

"Huh. I saw someone standing on the beach gazing at the horizon. It looked just like you."

Hannah laughed. "With all the tourists in town, I'm sure there are several other women who are my height with long brown hair."

"I suppose so, but you have that funny quirk of pulling on your braid and that's what this person was doing." He shrugged. "I suppose I was hoping it was you coming for a visit to my boat. Alone." Cal grinned.

Something in Cal's words made the hair on Hannah's neck rise. "Can you see if Meg needs any help at the snack bar? I have to check something."

"Are you all right? You look a little pale." He touched her arm gently.

Hannah walked to the door. "I'm fine, but there's something important I need to do."

"It sounds mysterious." Cal tried to lighten the mood with his tone but Hannah walked right past him toward her new cottage.

Was she crazy or did Cal just give her the key to the mystery?

Her hand lingered on the doorknob of her new cottage. If she didn't go in, if she didn't find what she expected, if nothing changed from this moment going forward, could she save anything? Or would the suspicion eat at her forever.

She rubbed Great Aunt Caroline's ring.

Hannah walked into her new cottage.

Dread filled every corner of her body.

With determination, she walked to the drawer in her kitchen and yanked it open. She stared at the iPad lying exactly where she'd left it.

Her hand shook as she reached for it.

CHAPTER 24

"I don't remember leaving my iPad here."

Hannah's fingers tensed around the device. "This one isn't yours, is it, Mom? You brought Dad's here earlier by mistake. That's why all the photos you took of me and Ruby weren't on it. They're only on yours. Dad didn't erase anything at all, did he?"

"Give it to me, Hannah. Adele has done enough damage to our family."

"And let an innocent person get blamed for her death? Is that what you want?"

"Of course not. It could just be the great unsolved mystery. Wouldn't that be a fitting ending for someone like Adele?"

Hannah clicked on the photo icon. She searched through the photos for one in particular. One taken of a person with her back to the photographer, her hair braided down her back as she stared out over the ocean. Anyone in Hooks Harbor could easily mistake the image to be Hannah.

But it wasn't.

"Moe thought he saw me near the marina early Saturday morning and Cal thought he saw me earlier today near the marina." Hannah looked up from the photo of her mother. "But it wasn't me they saw, was it? It was you. From a distance, from behind, we both look the same. You even pull on your braid the way I do."

Joanna backed away from Hannah, inching toward the open door. "Don't let Adele continue to destroy us, Hannah. With her gone, we can be a family again. That's all I ever wanted. For all of us to be happy."

"That's what Dad told me you said. What did you do?" Hannah could barely hear her own words. "What did you do, Mom?" she said louder. Anger flooded through her brain.

Joanna crumpled to her knees, her head in her hands. "I don't know. It all felt like a dream when I decided to take a walk on the beach. The air was still, the sound of the surf hypnotized me, and then I saw her. Adele. Standing next to that ridiculous sand sculpture of a mermaid. She laughed at me. Told me I was a terrible mother."

Hannah wanted to comfort her mother but her legs wouldn't move.

"Adele picked up the shovel and jabbed it at me. I don't know what happened after that, but the next thing I can remember is that I was staring down at Adele, lying dead in the sand. I panicked and ran down the beach. Somehow I ended up back in the cottage. Everything blurred together in a nightmarish slow motion scene."

Tears streamed down Joanna's face. "I didn't mean to do it. It was an accident."

Hannah finally saw her mother for the broken, desperate woman she was and she sat on the floor next to her. Joanna leaned on Hannah and sobbed.

"When did Dad get back to the cottage?"

Joanna shrugged. "I don't remember. I heard the door open and close but I don't know what time it was. I kept my eyes closed so he would think I'd been there the whole time, asleep."

Hannah stood and pulled her mother up with her. "Come on."

"Where are you taking me?"

Hannah sent a text message to Jack while Joanna blubbered. She wrote, *tell Pam to meet me at the beach where Adele was found in about thirty minutes.* She slipped the iPad into her sling bag and looped her arm through her mother's. "Come on Nellie."

Nellie woofed, always ready for anything.

Hannah's mind raced with possibilities as she drove with her mother sitting silently, staring out the window. Of course, the scene that screamed at her the loudest was that her mother murdered Adele. But she had to know for sure. She pulled into the marina parking lot.

"Why are you taking me here? Is this some kind of torture? Make me relive my horrible crime?" Joanna's eyes were wild and she picked at the sleeve of her shirt.

Hannah turned sideways in her car to face her mother head-on. "Listen to me, Mom. You just told me you don't remember what happened. Let's walk down the beach. Try to remember everything that comes back into your memory up until you argued with Adele."

"I don't want to. I only want to think about spending time with you and Ruby and getting to know sweet Olivia better. I don't want to relive that night."

"Don't you understand? Unless you know exactly what happened, you'll never be able to move on. It's all in the details." Hannah got out of her car and walked around to her mother's side. "Let's go."

Hannah waited next to the open door. Joanna stared straight ahead toward the ocean. "I remember looking out at that view when I walked down here. So peaceful."

Gently, Hannah held her mother's elbow and helped her to stand. Together, they walked away from the marina to the beach.

"Close your eyes and listen to the surf," Hannah suggested. "Tell me what you feel and hear."

Joanna closed her eyes, trusting her daughter to guide her. "The breeze is warm on my face." She reached around and braided her loose hair to keep it out of her face. "I had to braid my hair that night, too. The wind kept blowing it all around."

Hannah put her arm around Joanna's waist. She matched her stride with her mother's.

"I hear birds. Are there seagulls flying over us?"

"Yes. There are always gulls flying over the beach."

"I didn't hear birds that night, only the crash of the waves on the beach. It wasn't too loud, just a nice steady rhythm. I felt at peace."

They walked another hundred feet in silence.

"Until—" Joanna said. Her body tensed under Hannah's arm.

"What happened, Mom?"

"*She* started yelling at me. I didn't even know she was standing by her mostly-washed-away mermaid sculpture." Joanna stopped and put her hands over her ears. "It was awful. I didn't want to hear what she said. And then—"

"What did Adele do, Mom? Did she attack you?"

"I closed my eyes. I didn't even want to see her but she jabbed me with something."

Hannah's heart raced. Would her mother remember hitting Adele with a shovel? Was this a terrible mistake, bringing her back to this horrible memory? Forcing her to relive it?

Joanna suddenly reached both hands out in front of herself. "I grabbed the end to try to make her stop."

Hannah held her breath.

"When I opened my eyes, I was holding a shovel and Adele was lying on the sand."

"Dead?"

"I didn't wait to find out. I dropped the shovel. I panicked and ran back up the beach like I told you before. Back to the cottage."

Hannah put her hands on her mother's shoulders. "Was Adele lying in the sand face up or face down?"

Joanna closed her eyes again. She covered her bowed head with her hands. "She was face down." Her eyes opened. She stared at her daughter. "That doesn't make any sense, Hannah. How could she have landed face down if she was facing me? I wouldn't have been able to hit her in the back of the head."

Joanna hugged Hannah with a grip so tight she yelped. "I can hardly breathe," Hannah managed to get out.

"How did you know to make me relive that horrible night?"

Hannah sucked in a deep lungful of sweet oxygen. "A hunch. I didn't know what you would remember but there were too many people on the beach early Saturday morning besides you. Everyone had a slightly different version of events, but one person kept adding bits to the story. Always suggesting someone else as the potential murderer."

"Hannah!"

Nellie woofed and loped toward Jack.

"Why in tarnation did you have us come all the way down here? I'm an old man. Are you trying to give me a heart attack?"

Hannah smiled. Jack's curmudgeon talk didn't upset her anymore. She suspected he was after a compliment and she happily gave it. "That'll be the day. You're in better shape than the rest of us."

Pam huffed behind her father. She put her hands on her thighs until her breathing returned to normal. "Are you going to tell me what's going on? Why am I here, Hannah? It better be good. Did you find some important evidence?"

Hannah glanced at her mother. "Another piece to the puzzle...hopefully it will lead you to the last piece."

Pam frowned. "It better be good. I was just about to have a late lunch when Dad called."

Hannah winked at Jack. She suspected that Pam wouldn't have rushed to the beach if Hannah called, but she did take her father seriously. "I have a theory that there is a strong possibility of the existence of another shovel. The murder weapon."

"I already have the murder weapon. Adele's blood is all over Rory's shovel," Pam said without even trying to hide her annoyance.

"My mother argued with Adele just before she was killed. Adele jabbed her with a shovel. I think it was her *own* shovel that she used. Where is it?"

Pam clenched her jaw. "That doesn't make sense. How do you know?"

"Watch this." Hannah pretended to jab Joanna with a shovel. "How did you grab the shovel, Mom?"

Joanna closed her eyes, reached her hands out, and grabbed an imaginary shovel handle.

"Use your imagination for a minute, Pam. While my mother tugged on the handle with her eyes closed, Adele fell to the ground, face down. Adele didn't let go until she fell, which had to be *after* someone hit her from *behind* with a different shovel." Hannah flopped on the sand to demonstrate Adele's prone position at Pam's feet.

"This is a new twist on the facts surrounding Adele's murder. But what evidence is there to support your mother's story?" Pam turned toward Joanna, "No offense, Mrs. Holiday, but you've just admitted to being here and struggling with Adele. Without a witness, it's your word against, well, someone who can't testify."

Hannah interrupted. "Find another shovel, Pam. Rory's is accounted for. Adele didn't hit herself over the back of her own head. There has to be another shovel."

"Possibly." Her eyes darted around the scene.

"Did you see anyone else, Mrs. Holiday?" Pam asked. "Anyone for me to focus on to corroborate your story?"

"It was dark still, and I had my eyes closed until I saw Adele on the ground. I turned and ran."

"I'll follow you back to your place, Hannah. I want to see those photos you said you have, and I have a few more questions for your father," Pam said.

Hannah could only hope that Pam was trying to reconstruct the murder as she had described it. If Joanna's memory was accurate, a *big if*, finding another shovel made sense *and* it would clear her mother's name.

The alternative was not anything Hannah even wanted to consider.

Hannah and her mother drove toward the cottages.

"You never actually answered Pam's question, Mom."

Joanna turned her head to face her daughter. "What question? I answered everything."

"You said it was dark but you didn't say whether you did or didn't see anyone else near Adele." Hannah's eyes stayed on the road but she heard a short intake of air from her mother. "*Did* you see anyone else? Yes or no."

Silence.

"You did, didn't you? You saw someone."

Silence.

Hannah pulled in next to her father's rental car. When she opened her door, she could see that someone had packed most of her parents' belongings in the back.

"You and Dad are planning to leave that soon, huh?" Hannah looked over the top of her car toward her mother.

"As soon as possible."

"You both had me fooled except for one mistake. You said Adele was face down in the sand and Dad told me she was face up. How could that be?"

"I don't know what you're talking about." Joanna started to walk away but Luke was approaching and she froze.

"Where have you been, Joanna? I told you to stay away from Hannah. She twists everything to her advantage."

"Dad. When you saw Adele, how did she look?"

"Don't answer, Luke. Hannah is trying to trap you into saying something." Joanna's voice was filled with desperation.

"You *do* think I killed Adele. I can't believe it." Luke looked at Hannah. "When I saw Adele, she was crumpled in the sand. Her blond hair was all bloody. I couldn't believe what I was seeing." His eyes filled to the brim and his voice quivered. "I picked her up and moved her away from the waves. I thought she'd like to lie next to her mermaid, looking at the stars instead of her beautiful face smashed into the sand."

Hannah carefully watched her father's face. If anyone could read it, she was the one, and what she saw and what she heard felt like he was speaking from his heart. But she wasn't sure any more about her mother's version of events.

Pam stood listening to Luke's explanation. "Don't any of you leave this town." She held her hands out. "Give me your keys for now and stay in your cottage until I get back."

Luke handed over his keys, put his arm around Joanna's shoulders, and the two walked slowly to *Something's Fishy*.

CHAPTER 25

Hannah called Nellie and together they drove to the library. She wanted to catch Karla while she was there volunteering. Hannah didn't know which Karla she'd find—the friendly, chatty Karla, or the angry, leave-me-alone one. Karla had shown both sides to Hannah.

Fortunately, the library was mostly empty and Karla was in the last stack, shelving books.

"Got a minute?" Hannah asked.

"Not really." Karla held a pile of books and methodically found the proper place for them, trying her hardest to ignore Hannah.

"Okay, then. I'll ask you about Adele's murder right here, then, if that's how you want to play the game."

Karla's eyes widened. "I'll take my break and we can stand outside. Five minutes is all I have."

"That's enough time."

Karla placed the pile of books back on the cart and told Monica she'd be outside for her break.

Once outside, she put her hands on her hips and faced Hannah. "What is it now? Every time I think I've seen the last of you, you pop up like a great white shark's fin ten feet from shore."

Hannah ignored responding to the comment but did like the image. "When my father gave you a ride early Saturday morning, did he give you anything?"

"Like what? Why would he give me anything?"

"Can I look in your bag?" Hannah pointed to a large satchel with a ton of pockets that Karla had slung over her chest.

Karla clamped her arm tight against her bag. "No."

Hannah counted to five. "Okay. Did my father give you something to wipe your hands on?"

"Oh, yeah, he did. Does he want it back?" Karla unzipped a pocket on the front of her bag and pulled out a handkerchief that had once been white. It had the initials LH embroidered on one corner. "I was planning to wash it first. I fell in the sand and used it to wipe my hands. I guess he didn't want me to get all the sand in his car."

Hannah took the handkerchief and noticed stains that could certainly be blood.

"Listen, I know what you're thinking, but those stains were already there when he handed it to me. Your father was weird, and as soon as I closed the door, I wished I never got in the car with him."

"Weird, how?" Hannah asked.

"All the talk about Adele, like he was talking about someone in the past. And his voice was shaky. I don't know. It was creepy. After I found her body in the morning, I thought of him and wondered, you know, did *he* kill her?"

"I don't think he did," Hannah replied with only the tiniest shred of doubt at this point.

"Of course you'd say that. He's your father." Karla started to walk back into the library. "Oh, I almost forgot. I've got something in the trunk of my car and I'm sick of hauling it around. I don't know what to do with it."

Hannah's ears perked up. She followed Karla to an old Honda Civic parked in front of the library and waited for Karla to jiggle her key in the lock until the trunk popped up.

"Moe asked me to take this the morning after we found Adele dead."

Hannah looked into the trunk. A shovel lay inside. "Is this Moe's shovel?"

Karla shrugged. "With this *A* on the handle, I'm guessing it was Adele's shovel."

"Adele's? Why would Moe have her shovel?"

Karla shrugged as if she couldn't care one grain of sand less. "A memento of their relationship?"

Hannah took it out and transferred it to her car along with her father's handkerchief.

"I've got to get back to work. Monica's kind of strict about my break time and I definitely don't want to get on her bad side." Karla rolled her eyes as if she and Hannah were somehow now buddies or something.

Hannah sat in her car and sent a text to Jack: *I'm at the library. Just talked to Karla. I have Adele's shovel. Let Pam know.*

Jack texted back: *be careful.*

This was getting crazier and crazier. Who was lying? She hoped it wasn't her mother or father, or Karla or Rory for that matter, which only left one person. And speak of the devil. As Hannah looked up from her phone, Moe was walking toward her car with a determined stride. He turned and took the library steps two at a time.

Well, well, well. She decided to stay put to see what he did when he came back out. Hannah's wait lasted as long as it took three cars to drive by.

Moe marched right over to Hannah's driver side window and smacked his hand on the glass until she rolled it halfway down. "You've got something of mine."

"I don't think so." She patted her pockets. "Oh, you're right, you must be referring to this." She pulled a crumpled up piece of paper from her pocket and handed it to Moe. "One of your cigarette butts. You can dispose of it properly."

He tossed the paper right back into Hannah's car. "Karla gave you something and I want it back." He reached through the open window and put his hand around Hannah's arm and squeezed. "Get out."

Nellie growled but Moe had the door open and pulled Hannah out, slamming it closed before Nellie could follow.

"You've been nothing but a pain in my life and I'm ready to move on. Open the back."

Hannah fiddled with her keys, letting them slip through her fingers. She kicked them farther under the car.

"You think you're pretty clever, don't you?"

Hannah heard the tension rising in Moe's voice. He looked around. He couldn't risk opening the back door to climb over the seat with Nellie barking furiously. He couldn't bend down and reach for the key himself without giving Hannah a chance to get away.

"I'm wondering one thing, Moe." She grunted when he twisted her arm behind her back. The shovel lay in plain view with a big *A* engraved at the top of the handle. "How did you switch Rory's shovel for Adele's."

"Shut up." He pushed her down on her knees. "Grab the keys."

Hannah reached under her car. "My arm's not long enough." She sighed with relief. Someone had to come by soon to hear Nellie barking and help her.

Moe crouched next to her without letting up his pressure on her arm. If he twisted any more the socket would pull apart, if that was possible. She rubbed her finger on her free hand over Great Aunt Caroline's ring. It focused her mind away from the pain.

She had to keep talking. Keep Moe distracted. "Adele criticized your work, didn't she?" Hannah knew exactly how Adele operated and how she could target someone's weak spots.

Moe's eyes blazed. "She wanted to destroy me. I can't believe I ever thought I could love someone that was such a narcissist."

Hannah suspected that comment was accurate for both Adele and Moe but she decided not to point out that fact at the moment. Obviously, Moe didn't see his own shortcomings.

Moe pulled Hannah to her feet. "Come on." He kept his grip on her arm as tight as a vise as he pulled her down the sidewalk.

Hannah felt panic rising in her chest. She twisted but he only squeezed harder and kept her moving away from her car. "Where are you taking me?"

"The tables are turned now, aren't they? You'll be my ticket out of this dump of a town."

Moe shoved Hannah over the driver seat of his Jeep Wrangler onto the passenger seat, never releasing her arm. He took a deep breath. He had to fumble in his pocket to slip the key out with his left hand and reach over to start the Jeep. It was awkward, to say the least, and in his panicked state, he couldn't get the Jeep started.

"You won't get away, you know."

"It was perfect. I found Rory's shovel and I knew Adele would be sitting with her stupid mermaid." Moe looked at Hannah. "I bet you didn't know that she actually fancied that she was a mermaid in another life." He shook his head. "That should have tipped me off to her personality but, no, I got sucked in by her beauty."

"And my mother showed up at the perfect time. You couldn't have planned it better if you tried," Hannah said.

"You know? Adele tried to hit your mother. I should have let them finish each other off but I felt Rory's shovel in my hand and swung it. Adele went down with one hit. Your mother looked down at Adele's body and ran off. I guess she never even saw me."

"So, in a roundabout way, you protected my mother. Adele might have killed her if you hadn't been there."

Hannah felt Moe's grip on her arm relax slightly.

"I guess you're right. Who knows what Adele would have done?"

"Why did you take her shovel? Why not just leave it there?"

"Nothing against Rory, but he had a motive so when I saw his shovel, I grabbed it and used it. I rubbed his shovel in the blood and took Adele's. Seemed like a good plan at the time." Moe stared at Hannah. "I would have gotten away with it, too. Except for you. Always asking questions. Always moving closer. I should have dealt with you the first time I saw you."

His Jeep roared to life and Hannah's heart started sinking.

Hannah scanned the road. She knew the town and Moe didn't. "Watch out!" she shouted as he almost pulled out in front of a car driving past. Instinctively, Moe let go of Hannah's arm to shift, and when he slammed on the brakes, she used the moment of freedom to jump out of the Jeep.

She ran back toward her car, glancing over her shoulder, hoping he wasn't pursuing.

She stopped and relief flooded her body.

Deputy Pam Larson's cruiser blocked Moe's Jeep. His escape was over.

Hannah's knees buckled and she had to lean against a parked car, sliding down as her legs gave out. What would he have done to her? She shuddered at the thought.

Footsteps rang in her ears from both directions.

"Hannah. Are you all right?" Jack's voice sang out. "Fortunately, Karla called her mom in a panic and she let me know that Moe was dragging you down the street."

She nodded.

Cal crouched next to her. "I can't let you out of my sight for two seconds anymore," he teased as he pulled her close.

Karla appeared in front of Hannah. Her eyes were wide and her mouth hung open. "What happened? Moe was furious when I told him I gave you that stupid shovel and I said to myself, serves her right for being such a pain in the neck with all the questions. But I never thought he'd hurt you. I'm really sorry. And I almost ran off with him to Florida?" She shook her head. "I can't believe how stupid I've been."

Nellie managed to squeeze out the half-open window of Hannah's car. Before she could put her hand up, her whole face was slathered with dog slime. She wrapped her arms around Nellie's neck and breathed in the comforting doggy scent.

A small crowd grew around Hannah as the grapevine in town worked like a tsunami. Meg and Samantha pushed through some gawkers.

"What have you gotten yourself into now, Hannah?" Meg's gruff voice asked, barely hiding a tremor in her words. "And before you even ask, we locked up the snack bar to get over here as fast as possible. You're way more important than a few lost sales of clam chowder and fish and chips."

Samantha nodded in agreement. She was uncharacteristically quiet, choked up most likely, as she put her hand on Hannah's head.

The crowd parted, opening a path for Deputy Pam Larson to reach Hannah.

"I do need to ask you some questions. Can you come to the station? My biggest wish at the moment is to give this creep everything he deserves as quickly as possible."

"I'll drive her." All heads turned toward the deep voice. Luke held his hand out to Hannah. "If that's okay with you."

Hannah wiped her eyes with the back of her hand. The surge of adrenaline that overloaded her body moments earlier was seeping away, leaving room for her emotions to take over. She nodded and took her father's hand.

Nellie refused to leave Hannah's side which was fine with her. Luke started to protest when Hannah opened the back door of his rental car for her loyal companion, but changed his mind and kept quiet.

Hannah sank into the passenger seat, rolled the window down, closed her eyes, and let the wind blow over her face. Her mind needed these few minutes to relax before the difficult rehashing of the events with Moe were dredged up, front and center. Even her father's company and quiet voice comforted her.

Luke cleared his throat. "So, I think we should still have the pool game."

"Fine."

CHAPTER 26

Hannah huddled with Jack, Cal, and Meg at The Fishy Dish to work on a strategy for her pool game with her father. Luke insisted that the game be played before he and Joanna left town.

"Just tell him no," was Meg's suggestion.

"I agree," said Jack. "You don't need an excuse. So what if he gloats?"

"A deal's a deal. I'm playing the game."

"You know him best, but I want to be on record saying I think it's a terrible idea." Jack walked away from the counter in The Fishy Dish's kitchen, shaking his head.

Cal drove Hannah to the Pub and Pool Hall where everyone had agreed to meet at four. "Just walk away from the game. You can't risk losing."

"Thanks for the vote of confidence, Cal. I thought, you, at least, would be on my side." Hannah felt the pressure and it didn't help that every single one of her friends, along with her sister Ruby, told her she was making the biggest mistake of her life.

"I *am* on your side. That's why I want you to change your mind."

"I can't. I have to do this or I'll regret it forever. Besides, he'll see me backing out as a forfeit and he'll think he gets the land anyway."

They rode over the potholes in silence.

Luke's rental car was in the parking lot, alongside Meg's rust bucket. At least she didn't have to ride in that, Hannah said to herself. She reached across the seat and put her hand on Cal's arm. He released the wheel and squeezed her hand. "You'll win. I can feel it in your confidence."

Hannah smiled. She *was* confident. This was a turning point for her to leave some issues from her past right where they belonged. In the past.

Michael held up a mug as soon as Hannah entered. "Your favorite. Or do you want to wait until after?"

"I'll wait."

Hannah glanced at her father and nodded. Joanna sat by herself, looking lonely and forlorn. Her sadness wrenched Hannah's heart.

The pub felt more like a funeral home than a pool hall but Hannah couldn't help that. At least, not until *after* the game.

Luke had the balls racked up and he handed Hannah a cue stick. She chalked it. "My normal shot." She used her cue stick to point to the solid ball at the corner of the rack and the far pocket.

Hannah's flip flops slapped on the floor as she walked around the table. It was the only sound breaking the eerie silence.

Her break was perfect and she sank the solid ball just as she predicted. With careful deliberation, she walked around the table and made three more shots before she missed.

An eruption of groans weighed heavily on Hannah's shoulders.

Joanna stood to get a better view, both hands flat on her chest. Luke sank four balls, then missed. His touch was off, Hannah noticed.

Whispering in the background barely registered in her brain as she chalked her cue stick, surveying her options.

She sank her remaining three solid balls, but left herself with an impossible shot to reach the eight ball and add this game to the winner column. She glanced at Cal. He smiled, letting her know she still had time to do what needed to be done. His support lightened her heart while she tried to be calm and wait for her father's turn to end.

Luke chalked his cue stick and walked around the table. He smirked. "I gave you a chance, but now it's all mine." He sank his remaining three striped balls. With only the black ball to sink, it looked like Hannah was doomed.

She held her breath.

All eyes stared at Luke.

Luke tapped the cue ball. It moved toward the eight ball. The eight ball rolled at a snail's pace closer and closer to winning the game for Luke.

The eight ball sank out of sight in the pocket.

Everyone gasped except one.

Luke smiled.

The room exploded with noise and yells for a rematch. All eyes were glued to Hannah's face. She stood next to her father and looked around the room. "Dad won fair and square."

Luke raised his hand. "I've decided," he began, facing a roomful of angry faces. "I've learned something," he continued haltingly, "Hannah and Caroline's business belong together. My wish is to dedicate one of the guest cottages to Adele Bailey by naming the cottage *I'd Rather Be A Mermaid*." He paused. "Plus, make a large donation toward a memorial for her."

Mouths dropped.

Eyes blinked.

Then smiles bloomed on the faces staring at Hannah.

"And one more thing." Luke silenced the crowd. "Drinks are on me!"

Michael poured beers, wine, and whatever else anyone wanted. The noise level rivaled the surf at high tide during a storm. No one seemed to care that Hannah lost the pool game now that they knew she *didn't* lose her property.

"Nice game," Cal whispered in Hannah's ear. "Are you free Friday night to accept your winnings from *our* wager?"

"Hmmm." Hannah tilted her head back and forth, racking her brain, pretending she had a full calendar of engagements.

"There is an expiration date on the gift."

"In that case, Friday is perfect." She smiled and felt a contentment settle all the way to the tips of her toes. Rocking on the ocean in Cal's boat, her feet up, and stars flickering overhead was a date she never had any intention of missing.

"Great. I'll get you a drink. You've earned it."

She felt a hand on her back. "Clever. But you almost gave me a heart attack," Jack said. "When did you and Luke cook up that little surprise?"

"In the car on the way to the police station. When Dad realized how close he came to losing me, he sort of apologized for the last ten years." Hannah shrugged. "We're on the road back to being a family."

"Sort of?"

"I think his exact words were, 'I could have done better.'"

"It's a start. Caroline will be thrilled now that she doesn't have to worry about your father stealing your property."

"I do still have to make my mortgage payment," Hannah said. "Will she help me with that?"

"Of course, what else can she do with her money?" Jack grinned. "That I control, by the way." He stood quietly next to Hannah. "I have a question."

Hannah raised her eyebrows.

Jack leaned close to her ear. "Did you *let* him win?"

Hannah smiled. "My contribution to family peace. But don't you *dare* tell anyone."

Jack elbowed Hannah in the side and ran his thumb and finger over his lips, zipping them closed.

She knew she could count on Jack to keep a secret like no one else.

A Note from Lyndsey

Thank you for reading my cozy mystery, *Catch of the Dead.*

Never miss a release date and sign up for my newsletter here—http://LyndseyColeBooks.com

ABOUT THE AUTHOR

Lyndsey Cole lives in New England in a small rural town with her husband who puts up with all the characters in her head, her dog who hogs the couch, her cat who is the boss, and 3 chickens that would like to move into the house. She surrounds herself with gardens full of beautiful perennials. Sitting among the flowers with the scent of lilac, peonies, lily of the valley, or whatever is in bloom, stimulates her imagination about who will die next!

Drowning in Dahlias

Hidden by the Hydrangeas

Christmas Tree Catastrophe

Made in the USA
Coppell, TX
02 October 2021

63327697R00152